# BASQUE PEOPLE

BY DOROTHY CANFIELD

DECORATIONS BY ROBERT BALL

HARCOURT, BRACE AND COMPANY

NEW YORK

*Typography by Robert S. Josephy*
PRINTED IN THE UNITED STATES OF AMERICA
BY QUINN & BODEN COMPANY, INC., RAHWAY, N. J.

# CONTENTS

# BASQUE PEOPLE

## AT THE SIGN OF "THE THREE DAUGHTERS"

NE day in Itsasmendia we had a visitor from the great world. A Parisian acquaintance, moved by the skeptical curiosity of people who have seen too much, made the jolting way-train trip from Biarritz to judge for herself, she said, whether a Basque fishing-village was different from any other. By dinner-time she had found out, she informed us, that it was not.

Dining with us that same evening was an old Basque friend, the village school-teacher. She had been born and brought up in a remote Basque-speaking valley in the Pyrenees, had had a few years' training in a normal school of the region, and after that for twenty-five years had taught school in this little settlement of fishermen and small farmers tucked in between the Bay of Biscay and the Pyrenees. As you can see, she was but a provincial nobody. Wherever could she, I wondered, as I watched the two women together, have learned that easy naturalness of manner? And why in the world should she at fifty-five, rough, plain, lean, dark, unpowdered, unarranged, make the sophisticated woman of the same age, carefully tended and smoothed, seem like a wilted flower?

The conversation turned, naturally enough, on the Basques—the strangeness of their racial isolation, not only unrelated to the European Aryans all around them, but to any other of the races of mankind; their legendary vitality which has outlasted the Romans, the Goths, the Moors, feudalism, monarchy, industrialism; their passionate clinging to incomprehensible old folkways; the oddness of the fact that unlike all other peoples they never seem to have roamed and migrated to and fro, but (since they are probably descendants of the Pyrenean cave-dwellers) are the only human beings

4

in the history of our race who took root where they were planted.

Over our coffee I made the comment, "Doesn't it seem curious that so aged, aged a race should have so much more sap in its old stem, be so much more life-loving, than the younger nations around them? Why should they be far less afflicted by physical disease and moral lassitude than the rest of Europe . . . than the rest of the modern world? Why should they be the only ones who do not echo Europe's note of despair? What can be their secret?"

Before the words were out of my mouth, I knew exactly what the Parisian would answer. Every mention of the Basques pushes the same button in the French mind. Sure enough. Her response was their usual formula: "Isn't it strange that so old a race has produced no art? None. They have no great music, no great literature, not even decent pottery." She meant, evidently, "How can such a race presume to go on cumbering the earth?"

I expected an explosion, and a picturesque one, from the school-teacher, for she is a true fiery-hearted Basque, hotly, almost amusingly, proud of her race, and like the rest of her people has no patience with the drab

Anglo-Saxon notion that there is something indecorous about expressing honest emotion. But she made no protest. Said not a word. Responded only by an enigmatic smile and turned the conversation.

After we had gone with our out-of-town visitor to the station and had seen her on the ten o'clock train, we stood still for a moment, noting how mild was the lightly stirring air, how clear and soft the stars. It was the very night for one of our late-evening strolls back and forth along the footpath through a clover field on top of the headlands. Without even needing to propose this in words to each other, we turned into the steep cliff path, the loose stones rattling under our feet as we climbed.

When we emerged upon the table-land I was startled. . . . I always forgot—between those evenings on the cliffs. The distant lights of the Spanish coast were faint and yellow on our left; to our right Biarritz was a handful of white sparks; the dark sea breathed and whispered rhythmically far below us, the blossoming clover sent up in the starlight a fainting sweetness to mingle with the saltness of the sea-breeze. On a summer night there was, I thought, no lovelier spot on earth.

6

"How can any one," asked my friend with exquisite simplicity, "once having seen the Basque country, be content to live anywhere else?"

This was more like her. And it reminded me of my earlier wonder at her not picking up the French gauntlet. I asked her curiously, "What is in your incalculable Basque brain that you can smile, apparently with pity, when French people bring out complacently with their everlasting flourish their everlasting 'But the Basques have no art'? Even I get tired of hearing them say it. What un-Aryan idea lies back of your smile? What is it you think and do not say?"

She gave a little laughing murmur: "If I don't say anything to them it is because there is so much to say. And it would perhaps not be in very good taste for a Basque to say it to an Aryan. No art? No art among the Eskualdunak! Let me see if I can't think of a way to tell you what I thought and did not say to that Frenchwoman."

She walked beside me silently for several turns up and down the path, sometimes bending her head to look down at the clover-blossoms dim and sweet and dew-drenched, sometimes lifting her face to look up at the stars, so much brighter than the lights of Biarritz. Pres-

7

ently she began, "In my classes not long ago I had a little girl who was a foundling. . . ."

I perceived with enthusiasm that her answer was to be another of the stories from life heaped in her memory as in that of any deep-hearted woman who has taught twenty-five years in the same school.

She went on:

"The child had been sent years before as a tiny baby from the Paris office of the State Child-Placing Bureau, what we call the Assistance Publique. One of the aged traditions which we hold with our irrational, unenterprising Basque conservatism is that children are to be treated kindly. Our climate is a very fine one. As a consequence the French government sends to the Basque country a good many of the nameless foundlings for whom the state has made itself responsible. Our poor fishers and farmers see less cash in the course of a year than you would believe possible, so that the small sum paid by the state for the support of such children is welcome. There are always several such adopted boys and girls of unknown parentage in any Basque school. Everybody is used to them; they are treated exactly as well as their little Basque foster brothers and sisters. But that does not mean easy or even ordinarily comfortable lives. You have seen for yourself how little softness there is hereabouts for anybody . . . except for rich Aryan tourists, of course!

"Little Noémi had been taken as a six-weeks-old baby by one of our poorest families, the Hirigoyen, who have a small thin-soiled farm on a back road up towards Legarraldea. They tried to make no difference between her and the swarm of their own little boys and girls whether in food, clothing, work, or affection. But the foster child was not hardy enough for the food and work on which the little Basques throve and grew strong. She was often ailing. The Hirigoyens did what they could for her, gave her the best of their plain food, and put off the heavier jobs on the other children.

"Now as far as actual hard work goes, the easiest of the tasks on a Basque mountain farm is watching the stock as the animals feed, seeing that they do not break through the hedges or do not roam too far when sent up for the day to the unfenced mountain pastures. You've probably heard a lot of romantic gush about the picturesqueness of being herdsman to animals. For people who know nothing about sheep the very name of 'shepherdess' seems to have a sort of candy-like prettiness. They will talk to you by the hour, too, about Giotto and David and what not, and tell sentimental stories about the strength of character developed by the leisure for meditation. I've lived among a pastoral people all my life, and as a matter of cold fact I've never seen anybody yet who, if he got too much of it, didn't become either half idiotic or half insane or wholly degenerate. That's so well known among us Basques that we always try to divide up that work, turn by turn, among all the family.

"The Hirigoyens meant to do this fairly. But it was more evident all the time that the foster child did not have the strength for her share of other work. Almost without anybody's meaning it, little Noémi was the one who morning after morning went off with her bite of lunch to watch over the two cows, the calf, and the ten sheep. That meant, of course, that she was frightfully irregular at school, although, one eye on the quarterly visits of the State Inspector of Placed Children, they did send her down to the village often enough (or almost often enough) to comply with his far-from-strict rules about school attendance.

"After a year or so . . . naturally . . . even when Noémi came to school, her books did her little good.

The other children were dishearteningly ahead of her in lessons, and, their wits being sharpened by the give-and-take of group life, were even on the playground far beyond her poor grasp, which seemed to grow feebler as the child sank deeper into apathy. Those endless stupe-fying hours in mountain pastures, with no stimulus to call out the inner powers of a child, with nothing to do but to watch in a trance of imbecile idleness the hyp-notically recurring flash of sheep's teeth as they bite off blades of grass and then more blades of grass! When I was a little girl I took my turn at it. I know.

"I did my best for Noémi, giving her extra time during the noon recess and special attention in class. And once in so often, boiling hot within and without, I toiled up the mountain road to the Hirigoyen farm, intending to blow them sky-high. But I always cooled off when I saw the good folks working themselves like horses to make both ends meet. They were honestly try-ing to do the best they could. They throve on their cornmeal bread, sour milk, and hard work. But they were right about Noémi; she had not their stamina. It was a perplexing situation for them. There was no room in their world for an idler. They were really doing the child the greatest kindness in their power when they

11

gave her almost a monopoly of the easy job of loitering around the fields, watching the stock. At least it kept her pretty well physically. When I spoke about its making her stupid and backward, they told me seriously that Noémi was not very bright. She was a good child, they said; they all loved her gentle ways, but she certainly was not all there mentally. So, of course, it wasn't such a serious matter, they thought, if she didn't get much schooling.

"By the time Noémi had struggled along up to her eleventh year I began to think they were right, that she was not merely backward but definitely subnormal. On the days when she did come to school she sat stolidly at her desk during the recess and noon hours, refusing with a wordless shake of her head to go out to play, looking down at her hands, picking at her fingers, or, when she thought no one was looking at her, furtively eating bits of her lunch, always kept hidden inside her desk. I tried all my usual devices for arousing dull children— bright pictures, pretty little jobs of handiwork, collections of shells to play with. But nothing that I could do seemed to reach her. But of course, she was at school only once in a while, and with fifty-odd active imps in my class I have little time for any special one.

"We all saw her life plain before our eyes. She would grow up and always live on that remote mountain slope, silently serving the silent cattle, gentle, sluggish half-sister to the animals. Not an unhappy life for a halfwit, sheltered from the brutality of the world as she would be by the faithful affection of her Basque protectors. She was rather pretty, with delicate features and large soft eyes. We were all glad to know her out of the way of what city life does to helpless half-witted girls who are physically attractive. In the decent Basque world she would be at least quite safe.

"And then in a strange, backward way, a wonderful thing happened to her. A taint in her blood showed itself, one of those hereditary Aryan taints that seem strange to our Basque eyes. One of our stubborn and obstinate racial folkways is the habit of clean ancestors. A sore appeared on one of Noémi's knees, a little sore of which we thought nothing, no bigger than a boil. But it did not heal. For weeks it grew larger and deeper and more angrily full of pus. She was more and more often absent from school, and finally I went storming to blow the Hirigoyens up for no longer even going through the motions of sending her to her classes. I

13

found her bedridden, lying in a corner on a mattress, dumb and unprotesting as a sick animal.

"So I blew up in other directions. It took a good many explosions, but I did at last sufficiently blow up the Inspector and blast away enough government red tape to get her moved to the free ward in the hospital at Bayonne. Do not imagine that this was accomplished as easily as I have told it. I encountered nothing but opposition in every direction. Not from Noémi herself. She was morally too numbed and physically too sick to notice what happened to her. But the Inspector, buried deep in official *paperasses* as he was and overburdened with work, was almost impossible to stir. And the Hirigoyen, with the rooted country suspicion of hospitals, fought hard against her going and when she was carried out of the house were sure she was being taken to her death and cried like children.

"Her trouble was serious, they said at the hospital, serious but by no means incurable. With good care thereafter she might never have it again. The treatment—mostly perfect rest in bed, hearty food, and long sun-baths—would take many months.

"The Inspector of Placed Children groaned at the thought of the new red tape involved, the endless blanks to be filled out and reports to be written in duplicate and sent to the Paris office to cover and justify all this. I left him groaning and went back to tell the Hirigoyen. Not a cheerful visit, I assure you, as they had no doubts she was being held in the hospital for dissecting purposes and covered me with reproaches to fit.

"They were of course too poor and too Basque to think of taking the long trip (all of fifty miles) into the ravening metropolis of Bayonne (all of twenty thousand inhabitants). For a week we heard nothing. Then the Inspector had a report from the hospital, made out on the proper official blank, to the effect that 'the Hirigoyen child was in as satisfactory condition as could be expected.' He passed this on to me when I asked him the news. I asked him if he had been to see her. He was a conscientious official, but at this question he flung his arms up over his fatigued gray head. 'Me! Single-handed, with three hundred and twenty-two government foundlings in my district. Good God! The paper work—let alone the regular quarterly visiting . . . !'

"So the first chance I had, about a fortnight after she'd been taken away, I went to Bayonne myself. At the hospital I was astonished to have the Sister in charge of visitors tell me that she thought I would not be allowed to go in.

" 'Me . . . not allowed to go in!' said I, bristling, for Sister St. Teresa, grand though she might look in her black robes and white coif, was no other than she who had been the youngest of the eleven Sallaberry children, whom I had dragged up through the multiplication table and the alphabet and knew as I knew the inside of my pocket.

"Sister St. Teresa backed down a little and brought Reverend Mother to explain. The explanation was preposterous. . . . That very afternoon, she told me, another lady called, asking to see little Noémi Hirigoyen. It was the regular visiting day. She had been allowed as a matter of course to enter. What happened nobody knew, for nobody had chanced at that time to go out on the sun-terrace where Noémi's little bed was placed. But suddenly the lady visitor had rushed through the ward and out of the hospital, her handkerchief at her eyes, sobbing convulsively. And at the same time hysteric shrieks from Noémi sent a Sister running to her.

"But not a word of explanation was to be had out of the child.

" 'What did the lady do to you?' she had been asked, again and again.

" 'Nothing. Nothing,' sobbed the child. 'She just looked at me. It frightened me so!'

"A Sister was with her now, trying to quiet her down. And naturally, I must understand, they doubted the wisdom of letting her receive another visit.

" 'Now, Reverend Mother,' said I, using my most high and lofty old-teacher tone, when she had finished this tale, 'let me tell you something. Somebody in your hospital is playing horse with you. Not a word of all this can be true. I know all about that child. Except to come to my school and to go to church, she has never till now been off the Hirigoyen farm. Nobody outside of our village has ever seen her. It is simply impossible that any "strange lady" can have known there was such a child, let alone have known that she is here.'

"At this, Reverend Mother looked at me hard. 'Isn't she a foundling child? From the Assistance Publique?' she asked. 'And isn't it the rule of the Paris office to notify the mother of what happens to those children if the mother wishes it?'

"I fell off my high and lofty tone in one tumble. Till that moment I'd clean forgotten that Noémi did not belong to the Hirigoyen by blood. She'd been with them, you'll remember, since she was a tiny baby. We stood staring at each other silently.

" 'Well,' said Reverend Mother finally, 'we'll let the little girl herself decide if she feels like seeing you.'

"Of course Noémi sent out for me at once. As I went in, Reverend Mother cautioned me not to excite her. But I found the child excited enough already. Strange to find agitation on the little face I had always seen so heavy and dull! She had told the Sister that she had been frightened. But in her startled eyes I saw more than fright. She had had a great shock, evidently, but had it been altogether a painful one? I thought not, though on seeing me she burst again into loud tears and told me all over again about the strange lady who had appeared by her side and had looked at her. . . .

" 'Didn't she say *any*thing, Noémi?' I asked. 'And how was it she looked at you? What made you cry?'

" 'She looked . . . she looked . . .' said the child, but she found no words.

" 'What did *you* do, Noémi?'

" 'I looked back. I couldn't do anything else. And when her mouth and all her face began to tremble, I began to shake all over, too. And when she began to cry, oh!—oh!'

"Yes, it had done more than frighten her. There was more than panic in the tears which now once more poured from the child's eyes. I had never seen her cry before. I had not dreamed her capable of such feeling.

"She grew quieter as I turned the subject, gave her the flowers I had brought, and began to tell her bits of home and school news. But when I rose to go, the agitation in her eyes flickered up again. She pulled me down to her pillow and whispered in my ear, *'The lady kissed me.'* With that she began to weep loudly again, burying her face in the bedclothes. I had never thought that anything in the world would make me positively enjoy seeing a child cry.

"Yes, of course, as you knew at once, it was her mother. And a week or so after this, her mother and I met at the hospital (Reverend Mother arranged this and sent for me) and had a long talk. The mother had been, it seemed, born and brought up in a mountain hamlet not far from my own old home. There's no need to tell you the details of her story, for it is a familiar one to every member of the human race, Aryan or otherwise. A family of French tourists spent some weeks in her village the summer she was sixteen, and persuaded her, considerably against her parents' wishes, to go back to Paris with them as chambermaid. Like most young Basque girls, she was pretty. There was a grown son in the family. Now you know all you need to know except that, though the childish little exile was half-mad with fright and sorrow and homesickness and shame, she did not gladly seize on the opportunity offered her by the Assistance Publique to rid herself once and for all of the burden of her nameless baby. No, from the moment she knew she was to be a mother, she loved her child with that invincible naturalness of human feeling which is, of all qualities, what we Basques most prize, most cling to. Sheer penniless poverty and terror of the world forced her to leave her baby-girl in the hands of the state, but she begged the Assistance Publique official to place the child in a Basque family where she could be close to it, and to inform her of any change in its life. As she had passionately kissed the little thing good-by she had thought, 'perhaps . . . sometime . . .'

"She had come home to the Basque country, not to her own village, but to Biarritz, because it seemed to

her like a big city where she would have more chances
for employment and could recover her health and poise
among people who did not know her. Being decently
educated, with a good head for figures, and now very
sobered and serious, she had secured, on trial, the position of assistant to the cashier in a prosperous butcher-
shop. The work was poorly paid, and the hours long.
But she wanted no more soft positions in families. She
had at least now her own mansard attic room with a
key in the lock.

"Soon after she had begun to work there the proprietor of the shop died, and his only son, just back from
military service, inherited the business. He was as
Basque as his name of Ganich Etchevery, as Basque as
a *pelote fronton*. From his round, dark head to his
nimble sinewy *espadrille*-clad feet, he lived zestfully
up to every Basque tradition. What traditions? Well,
he played on the best *pelote* team of his part of town,
he was very devout, he was full of the high spirits of
exuberant good health, sang bass in church every Sunday, always made a point of smoking tobacco smuggled from Spain (you know we Basques do not at all
admit the right of the French government to shut us
off by customs and duties from our Basque brothers

who happen to live in Spain), was sound as a nut physically and morally, preferred cornmeal bread to wheaten, never wore a leather shoe, never walked abroad without a *makhila* in his hand, and felt very sorry for every one who was not of his race. He approved highly of the pretty, pure-blooded young Basque girl, so mannerly and retiring. And so did his family. All Basques know about each other's families more or less; there are so few of us and we have connections scattered everywhere. They knew of hers, respectable mountain farmers, tilling the soil which had been in their family for hundreds of years. Among other alien traditions most Basques have not adopted is the warm-hearted romantic Aryan institution of the dowry. It did not occur to Ganich to insist on having money with his chosen bride. In six months they were man and wife.

"'. . . And I hadn't told him! I meant to. I tried. Honestly. But I didn't dare. He isn't that kind of man. I knew he wouldn't understand. He had always lived with his mother and sisters . . . such good girls. One of them is a nun. He was so sure of me. I knew he'd never get over it if I told him. I didn't dare. . . . I was so crazy about him then. I am still! We have a

little girl now . . . seven years old . . . a darling.
Suzanne is her name, after my mother. It was his idea
to name her that. Wasn't it sweet of him? I have been
so happy. But always unhappy too, so ashamed I was
such a coward. I couldn't forget my little Noémi. I
knew all the time where she was. I tried and tried to
think of some way of going up there to Legarraldea to
see her. But what excuse could I give my husband? It
would take two days to go and come. Then they sent
me word from the Paris office that she was in the hospital here. I have a married sister in Bayonne, and I
often come over from Biarritz on the trolley to see her.
So I came. . . . I meant just to glance at her and pass
on. But when I saw her . . . my own little daughter
. . . she looks so like *us* . . . exactly like my little
sister who died . . . ! Now I have seen her I can never
let her go, never! She needs her mother! But how can I
. . . what can I do?'

"So we two Basque women put our heads together to
plan. After a time we went to see the Inspector, who,
after endless misery over the miles of red tape involved
in any change, agreed to what we had worked out . . .
at least temporarily. The state, in France, always
stands ready to restore foundlings to either parent at

any time it can be shown it is for the child's interest. Mme. Etchevery found a discreet, respectable family in a suburb of Bayonne who agreed to take Noémi after her treatment at the hospital was over. Here she could have good medical care, could go to school regularly, and here her mother could see her several times a week as part of her visits to her married sister. You may be sure that all this time I kept strictly to myself—not out of any delicacy or kindness but from simple cowardice —the unpleasant fact that Noémi was subnormal in intelligence. Her mother would learn that for herself fast enough, I thought.

"But it turned out to be something her mother never learned at all. Even before the end of her six months' stay in the hospital a new Noémi began to emerge. The life in her ward was so quiet and monotonous that it would have seemed to a Paris street child like being buried alive. But it provided a constant series of stimulating experiences to the little girl who had been limited to the society of sheep. The cleanliness, the order, the good food, the brief talks between doctor and nurse on the daily medical round, the reading aloud of a Sister during the meals, the comings and goings of other human beings, the echoes from the life of the big world

outside the hospital walls—above all, the frequent visits from her mother, focusing a passionately attentive
and ingenious affection upon her benumbed little personality—all these new life-elements woke Noémi
from her stupor. A child we had never seen looked about
and began to draw the breath of life.

"By the time Noémi's knee was quite healed and she
was moved to her new suburban home, the Hirigoyen
would scarcely have recognized her. And a year later,
after months of reasonably normal family life and
school, anybody who had ever seen her herding her
sheep would have scouted the idea of any connection
between this pretty, animated child and that little
earthen clod.

"Through my frequent reports, the Hirigoyen followed her progress, enchanted, incredulous! Noémi
standing high in her classes. Noémi taking first prize
for embroidery. Noémi with a gold filling in one tooth,
just like M. le Curé! Noémi learning to cook on a real
cook-stove, not over a hearth-fire! The day—what a
day!—when I told them that Noémi had begun to take
lessons on the piano . . . what a sensation on the side
of Mendigaïna mountain! Such shoutings to and fro!
'Gratien! Maria! Mimi! Our Noémi is taking lessons

on the piano! Where's Jeannot? In the cowshed? Run quick, somebody, and shout to him that Noémi is taking lessons on the piano!'

"In their pride and pleasure there was no alloy, except that she was lost to them. 'Of course she's much better off. But I miss her. I'm lonesome for her,' said Maman Hirigoyen, who had but nine of her own to keep her company.

"Noémi's mother, never having had any notion that the child was subnormal, naturally felt none of the astonishment which gave a special sweetness to our joy. That the little girl should develop and blossom out seemed natural enough to her. What seemed unnatural to her, increasingly hard, every day more sad, was the separation from the child who was every day dearer to her. And what was more than hard and sad, what was intolerable, was the shame of deceiving her husband. 'I can't look him in the face,' she told me bitterly as we chanced once to meet in the home where she had placed Noémi. 'It makes me sick when I tell him I am going to Bayonne to see my sister. And when I make up my accounts wrong, putting down that I have spent for dresses money that I've spent on Noémi . . . I *despise* myself! I'm in a trap and I can't get out!' Indeed the expression on her comely face, so plainly meant for sweet and simple happiness, was truly of despair.

"If there is one thing, old maid that I am, that I know nothing about, it is married life. It was absurd of me to dream of giving her advice. But we Basques act on impulse rather than reason. I remember that once I cried out to her, quickly, before I should have to think, 'Mme. Etchevery, there is nothing in your heart but love . . . bewildered though it may be. Why do you take for granted that your husband's heart is any less warm than yours? Why don't you tell him?'

"She turned very white, but she did not look surprised. I could see that she had thought of it before. 'Even if he put me out in the street,' she said slowly, 'I would respect myself more than now.'

"But I was sure she would never do it. It was so evident that all her life depended on her husband. She was frightened to faintness by only thinking of the possibility that he might cease to love and respect her.

"And yet one hot day, in the middle of the second summer after Noémi had gone away, when I had not seen Mme. Etchevery for a long time, there came a knock on my door. I got up sleepily from my afternoon siesta to answer. There she stood, her face as bright as a peony. She had evidently meant to greet me in a correct, citified way, for as I opened the door she was extending a gloved hand. But at the sight of me, I suppose at the associations brought up by my appearance, she gave instead a wordless cry and flung her arms around my neck.

"Of course I knew at once what she had come to tell me. But in my all-knowing wisdom I tolerantly decided to seem not to have guessed, and to let the simple-hearted creature tell me for the sake of the satisfaction it would give her. Then as she talked I found that I was about as near to all-knowing wisdom as life ever ironically brings me. For through her incoherent exclamations and excited, half-finished sentences something startlingly unexpected emerged.

"There had come to her, I gathered, a time of really desperate perplexity and unhappiness. She was beside herself with the horror of her own lying, and terrified because it seemed to her that her husband began to suspect her, peered at her furtively when he thought she was not noticing. 'I could not stand it any longer . . . I could not *stand* it. And yet my courage was not a bit greater. One night in bed—it was all dark, I did not

even know if he woke or slept—I made a prayer to the
Virgin to help me . . . and all at once, there in the
darkness was my own voice, very far from me . . .
speaking. I was terribly frightened to hear it! I cried, I
cried all the tears of my body . . . but the voice went
on . . . till . . . oh, you never could think what happened . . . never, never! I felt his arms around me,
my husband's arms, and his cheek as wet with tears as
mine . . . and then . . . it was not my voice, but his,
coming through the darkness . . . broken and falter-
ing like mine. . . . And what was it saying? Something he had never dared to tell me before . . . he had
been afraid of me—my Ganich! He had tried to tell
me before we were married. But I had seemed to him
too young, too ignorant of life. He was sure I could not
understand. All that time he had lived with a burden I
had not shared! My Ganich! And the trouble lately
had been that he thought I seemed absent and strange
in manner, that he feared I had learned . . . that I
was turning away from him in resentment. . . .'

"It was horrid, and sad, and sordid—what had happened to Ganich Etchevery at eighteen, when he had
been a shy, ignorant country lad, hot-blooded, awk-

29

ward, alone in Bordeaux for a time, and had given the
first flower of his youth to a worthless girl. She had let
him love her, had amused herself with playing on his
unworldliness, and then from one day to the next, had
flung off with somebody else (he had never known
who) to . . . he had never known where . . . Paris?
Lyons? Marseilles? She had amused herself for a few
weeks by tantalizing the distracted boy with messages
every day or so from a new city. He had understood
nothing of it all, had known nothing . . . not even
whether the child was his, the baby girl whom, months
afterward, she had cynically brought back to him one
night. As he came to the door of his room in answer to
a knock she had thrust the little bundle into his arms,
crying out mockingly as she disappeared into the street,
'She's yours! Better give her something to eat!'

"Before the stupefied boy could stir, he was alone
with the baby in his arms . . . he had never known
anything about it. '. . . My husband never even knew
surely that the child was his . . . and yet he took care
of her. Just a boy, and in such trouble . . . his first
great sorrow . . . but so deep-hearted even then. My
Ganich! Never was there such a heart! The little thing
in his arms was helpless and alone in the world. And he

did not let her fall. To have seen that she was fed and clothed, year after year, that was not enough for my Ganich. He went to see her regularly, had always given her time and thought . . . something of himself. Perhaps she really was his daughter. And even if she weren't, she had nobody but him.'

"Well, that was the warped, uncomely material which destiny gave those human hearts as stuff for their lives. From having read thousands of your English and French stories about what Aryan men and women do to each other, I know what a picture any Aryan writer would compose as the inevitable sequence of this explosion in their lives. If your artistic, greatly gifted story-writers tell the truth, here is the picture of what would have happened: the husband, even with good intentions, would have been mastered and overpowered by animal impulses of retrospective jealousy of his wife's past, hating—with all the force of subconscious instincts stronger than he—the child who was its visible reminder, spying on his wife's comings and goings with a poisonous suspicion of her every look and accent. The wife, as helpless as he before deep forces of evil in her nature, never able to forget that her husband had kept a secret from her for years, sick with a physical maternal jealousy of the child of another woman, unable to resist throwing up to him the uncertainty of its parentage, morbidly obsessed with the idea that the father favored that child, the other woman's. The three girls, so strangely flung together by life, reflecting disharmony, fishing with brutal self-absorption in these troubled waters to get all and give nothing, playing the weakness of one parent off against the weakness of the other—in short, hell on earth, the favorite theme, it seems to us Basques, of the so artistically gifted races around us when in what are called their great literary masterpieces they paint what they have seen, what they believe, of human relationships.

"What actually did happen? This unlearned butcher and the country woman who is the cashier in his shop, what did they make of this grotesque stuff of life haphazardly thrown at them, unexpected, disconcerting, shapeless? What did they create for themselves and the children dependent on them? To understand what they created, you must not forget that they are descendants of a race whose oldest tradition is that it is not only possible but natural for human hearts to give each other joy rather than pain and who recognize this as the natural and attainable end of human existence. Of a race which has never believed that 'art'—that fine-spun product created by a few mad egotists in each generation, acclaimed by a few, incomprehensible to most—is worth more than brotherly love and human happiness. Of a race which has never been taken in by the bragging claim of artists to be the finest specimens of humanity. A race which does not in the least agree that the production of an 'immortal' work of art—in fashion today, laughed at tomorrow, doomed to oblivion in a few centuries—is ample excuse for the sacrifice and misery of living human beings all around the artist. Of a race so old that it may perhaps—who knows?—have had time to try out "art" as an element of human life and to have turned away from it as a healthy man turns from the unreality of drug-pleasures. Or rather to have transferred it from the realm of color and line to that of human relationships. Why —we often feel like putting the question to Aryans— are the principles of art, so true, so fine, so deep, to be applied to everything save to human living? For us art is no fiery Moloch in whose red-hot belly our dearest and best perish to the tune of our demented rejoicings—no, we have outlived too many a breed of

33

Moloch-worshipers to . . . but I am beginning, I see, to talk Basque and not French. Let me get on with my story.

"As to what actually happened to the inartistic Basques of this particular story, it is a good thing that you do not need to rely on any testimony of mine, but can go and see for yourself. The next time you are in Biarritz, walk over into the old Basque quarter, to the fine big butcher-shop on the south side of the Port-Vieux. Step in and pay a call on the Etchevery family. Tell them you came from here, and they will be glad to see you. Ten minutes will be enough, all you'll need—far more than you'd believe if I told you. You won't see the children, probably (except the new little three-year-old), for they will be away at work or school. But you will find Ganich in his white apron behind his scrubbed, clean butcher's block. Take one long look into his quiet clear eyes. Madame, in her plain Basque black, will be at the cashier's desk. As she chats with you, watch her mouth and see how naturally its tender curves melt into the good smile, not to be imitated—is there a better in this world!—of a woman in security and at peace. You may, if you are lucky, catch a glance exchanged between them. That'll be something you'll like to carry away with you. Or one of them may chance to make a brief remark to the other. It will be in Basque. But you'll have no doubt as to its meaning.

"Then go out and look up at the brightly painted sign hanging over the door, and see the name they have chosen for the *enseigne* of their business—'*Aux Trois Filles.*' You may need to do a little meditating—in Basque perhaps—to take in all that that means, even when I have told you what Mme. Etchevery told me . . . the final saying of her husband that night, a saying full, it seemed to me, of clear sense of what are the true values, the real facts, of human life. He said at last to his wife, quite heartily and simply, 'Why, this is all it comes to. You and I are not different from what we were . . . after eight years of life together each knows who the other is, I should hope. And as to the rest . . . we had thought we had a poor little family of one small girl, and here we are rich with three daughters.'

"If you want to see what has become of those three daughters, go up with me next summer some day to the Hirigoyen farm. Yes, the poor little mountain farm on the road to Legarraldea. The Etcheverys have shown

35

as much warm natural understanding for the Hirigoyen as for each other. The mere facts of Noémi's hard life with her first protectors have not hidden from them the kindness of the farm family, fumblingly doing their poor best for the nameless child. Every summer Noémi is sent back (with many presents in her bag) to board with them for a month. Generally she brings her two sisters to run wild in the fields with her, for the three girls are inseparable comrades.

"Remember, I am not making any of this up. This is no literary story. It is just one of the things I have seen in my dull, uneventful life among an old race, very old, who have no art. And don't get the idea that these people are anything but quite ordinary . . . they are just a prosperous butcher with his country-bred wife, and a poor farmer with his ignorant family.

"What are the girls like? Well, Magdeleine, the oldest, the father's first child, nearly twenty now, is a fine hearty creature, not a bit clever, not very interesting, but strong and domestic-minded and warm-hearted. She's engaged to be married to a well-to-do young farmer of Arnéguy, up beyond St. Jean Pied-de-Port, a distant connection of Mme. Etchevery. She'll make a good mate for him and he for her. Little Suzanne was at first too much adored and spoiled by them all, but now that a baby brother has pushed her from the center of the stage she's a good little thing, just what a nice child of eleven ought to be. Noémi's the flower! Just wait till you see her! They're all so proud of her. She is past seventeen now and will be entering normal school in a year. For she is planning to be a teacher. Yes, she is planning to spend her life among our little mountain boys and girls. She said to me with her good laugh the last time I saw her, 'You see, I'm one of them. I'll be sure to know what they are up to.'"

The voice of my old Basque friend had sunk lower and lower to a murmur, and now she was silent. We had been walking slowly back and forth along the path through the clover field. The electric sparks of Biarritz still glared hotly on its rocky point. But the scattered lights on the distant Spanish coast had gone out one by one. The old sea drew its breath sighingly at the foot of the cliff. Back of us, black against the starlit sky, the Pyrenees rolled their dark bulk inland.

We stopped to look up at them, the shelter of the earliest ancestors of the woman by my side, the homes where her first forefathers had struggled to learn how to be men and not beasts.

She reached in the dark for my hand.

"Well? Well?" she asked me softly, a smile in her dark voice. "Do you see why I tell you this long, dull story? Can you guess what may be a reason why we of all races have never gone migrating from one corner of the globe to another? Why we have never been lured on by the idea that only three days' march away is the longed-for land where people can be happy and at peace without doing their share to create peace and happiness?"

I made a little protest: "But, dear friend, we Aryans are not *all* of us what our story-writers picture us. What you have been telling me—couldn't it have happened among simple people anywhere, among people where a quiet, uncomplicated life has not destroyed their sense of human values?"

She answered: "You asked me what was in my queer Basque mind that I can smile silently over the accusation that we have no art. Is it no art that, through all the countless ages of our life, we have kept ourselves clear of those complications which destroy the sense of human values? To have understood that human values are of more consequence than complications, and to have made the choice between them? No art? I'd like

38

to ask the people who say that—but they would never understand—is there nothing a human race can learn out of a long experience of life save how to paint lines on crockery pots? Is there no poetry that is not written but lived?"

## "VIVE GUIGNOL!"

 IFE in a military academy is no more regulated by authority than in a French school. Thus and no farther into the sacred precincts may parents penetrate when they lead the younger children to their classes in the morning. Here and no-where else must they stand humbly and wait at closing-hours till the children are released. It is as easy for a German or an Italian tourist to enter a French frontier fortress with a camera in his hand as for a mother to enter a French classroom to hear a recitation in arith-metic. In each case, if an authorization could conceiv-

ably be secured, it would come from no less a person than the head of a Ministry.

Everything in the school is foreordained by that distant potentate. His authority is steel-like and immutable. Minutely branching, it overlooks none of the minutiae of daily school routine. Every hour's work is laid out in advance: there is no appeal possible, no interruption of the schedule thinkable. How could a mere teacher in a little rural school reach the ear of the Minister of Public Instruction, and how presumptuous of her even to consider changing the program laid down by the highest and best of authorities!

And yet—those Basques! When their old traditions conflict with new ones, they just do as they like! For more than fifty years, the august Minister of Education was flouted in every one of the little schoolhouses scattered about in the narrow Pyrenean valley that holds the canton of Midassoa, where very little (save this invention of public schools) has been altered in the last two hundred years. Two hundred, do I say? A thousand!

Twice or thrice a year some child looked up from Napoleon's campaigns, or from the question of how much profit the baker would make if he sold bread for

one franc a kilogram, having bought his flour for six
hundred francs for a barrel weighing . . . from this
sort of consideration the child, raising his head, saw
opening before him a radiant vista of forgetfulness.
Down the road toward the school a gaunt old man
was trudging, his shoulders stooped under a great
wooden box, the black paint on which was as worn and
thin as the wayfarer's frayed clothes. The first child to
see him broke the penitentiary silence of the schoolroom with a shout, "Guignol! Here's Guignol!"—
sprang to his feet, and rushed out of the door, followed
by all his bullet-headed, black-aproned schoolmates,
tearing down the road, capering as they ran, and
shrieking joyfully, "Guignol! Here's Guignol!" Their
gladness poured like sunlight about the dingy old man.
His ancient, weary eyes brightened in that most inef-
fable of human joys, the certainty of being welcome—
rare in most lives, but the very substance of his. As
they swarmed toward him, children and grandchildren
of those who had raced with the same cries of welcome
to greet him years ago, he always set down his box and
stood by it to wait for them, a tremulous smile on his
lips. The children flowed about him, shouting shrilly,
plucking at his hands, jumping up and down, the big-

gest boys trying to lift and carry the magic chest between them.

At the door of the schoolhouse stood the teacher, as
forgetful of regulated routine as the children—forgetful too, for an instant, of her futureless life, living
again in her childhood when she too had burst from the
flat drab of everyday existence to race down the road
toward Romance, shouting "Guignol!"

The old man looked no older to her now than he
had then. He made her feel a little girl again, and it
was a little girl's smile that wiped from her face the
dark adult expression of conscientiousness.

If the day was fair the big box was set up and opened
in the courtyard of the school, just as, years before
there had been any schoolhouses in the Basque country,
it had been set up in the public square of the village.
If rain were falling, into the sacred classroom with it!
Push back the teacher's desk, usually as inviolable as
the Ark of the Covenant! Up with the creaking jointed
supports which had held it high this half-century and
more! "Children, sit down! Get yourselves settled. The
show is about to begin."

The old man took his place behind the box, threw
over the back of it and over his head and shoulders a

44

greenish-black cloth, and instantly, by tradition, became invisible, in spite of legs clad in threadbare trousers, supported by thin feet in ragged brown canvas
sandals.

A pause for arrangements within the theater; a pause
filled with thrills and wriggles and long breaths from
the waiting children—filled for the teacher with a gust
of perfume from her youth. A long arm came from
under the black cloth to pull a string which let down
the front of the box, and a scene was disclosed to the
eager eyes which recognized instantly the story that
was to go with it.

Was it a mill-wheel and some faded bushes painted
on the flimsy canvas backdrop? The children began to
laugh and clap their hands and shout out, "The Miller
and the Devil!" Was it a pasteboard castle with battle-
mented walls? "Pampelune! Roland and the Sara-
cens!" cried the boys. Did the backdrop show in
dimmed colors a row of gray stone houses with mansard
roofs and crudely painted ladies in crinoline promenad-
ing before them? "The new farce! The new comedy!"
cried the children. It had been new when the father and
mother of the teacher had sat cross-legged on the
ground to watch Guignol.

45

When the curtain, rolling up, revealed on the crumpled canvas a mountain gorge with pasteboard rocks strewn about the stage, it was not applause that burst from the children, but the strains of the immortal tune, "There *was* an old soldier, and he *had* a wooden leg." They were silenced by the appearance of the jovial, unregenerately profane old veteran himself, stumping on and exclaiming with gusto as he caught sight of his audience, "*Agur!* Children of the Eskualdunak! *Agur!* Just the friends I needed to see!" Then, advancing to the front, leaning forward with a confidential whisper: "What scrape do you think I've got myself into now?" To which the enchanted children answered, "You've been poaching again!" And "How in the world could you guess that!" from the old rascal on the stage.

There were no favorites. They were all favorites. The backdrop showing a tropical scene consisting of three green reeds and a strip of blue representing the ocean, which meant "Polichinelle and the Crocodile" and gales of laughter, was no more noisily welcomed than the painted marble pillars which were the background of the lamentable story of "The Countess and Her Lost Son," which always made the little girls cry.

46

If there was a favorite it was perhaps "Polichinelle and the Gendarme," and this was natural, because in the last act Polichinelle with a knotty club beat the wooden head of the gendarme till the echoes resounded and the younger children (to whom it was almost new) all but expired in their mirth.

In every story—at least in all the funny ones—the forces of law and order and morality were joyously outgeneraled, outmarched, and outwitted by delightful scalawags. Like the story of the endless triumphs of Robin Hood over the Sheriff of Nottingham, they were the expression of a folk oppressed by law-givers, forcing their cold, dry, logical morality hard upon the instinctive certainty of mankind that somehow you should be able to do as you wish without paying any penalty for it. The children's boisterous mirth laughed down, for a moment, the authority of the law-givers who ruled their lives so heavily. How they loved the naughty rogues who gave them this breathing-space! How heartily they scorned the stupidity of their victims! How idiotic of the rich old man who lent Polichinelle a bag of gold not to see the triumphant leer with which the latter favored the children, nor the limp stuffed forefinger laid cynically alongside the

47

wicked red rose, nor to hear the hoarse chuckle with which the impenitent hero let his audience know that he never intended to pay back a penny! The gendarme who, following out the obnoxious traditions of his trade, was trying to arrest Polichinelle for the murder of his wife, fell into one trap after another, was beaten to a pulp in ambuscades, was drenched with slops, and finally in the last act, chittering in terror, retreated from a ghost (impersonated by Polichinelle in a sheet), not seeing the jaws of the crocodile gaping behind him.

The little children always took hard hold of some one's hand during this exciting scene; some of them even, still naïve, moved to pity even for a gendarme, used to warn him shrilly, "Look out! Right behind you! Take care!"

The children, in fact, always took part in the action. The plays could not have gone on without them. At a critical moment Roland, leaning in his tin armor over a prostrate foe, used to ask squeakingly, "Shall I spare his life?" And was always answered by a thunderous "No!"

"Which way did the rascal go?" the gendarme would gasp out, rushing upon the stage just as Polichinelle, the inn-keeper's roast fowl under his arm, hid behind a chair. The children, in terror lest he discover their hero, cried out, "Out of the window into the garden!" or, "Down the street to the left!" After the baffled policeman had gone off on one of these false scents, how enchanting it was to have Polichinelle rise up slowly from behind his chair, waggle his head at them in triumph, and then, pirouetting madly with joy at his own duplicity, rush out to find the gendarme and play yet another trick upon him.

What golden lightness of heart filled the schoolroom during that hour of rest from the endless human strug- gle upstream toward its strange, hard, self-imposed ideals! What refreshment for those young souls as for an instant the grim insistence of civilization stopped grinding at them!

"I didn't suppose a little tap like that would kill her," remarked Polichinelle with no sign of regret, after having laid his wife low with a terrific blow from his club, "but" (carelessly) "she had a horrid voice and was always scolding; so it's just as well!"

Yes, yes, what a bright place the world seemed when one could get rid of people because they had horrid voices and scolded! Never, so long as the children could warn him in time, should the tiresome Law lay its talon on the defender of Freedom. How much more brilliant was the fun Polichinelle made for them than any they were to know in the conscience-ridden life before them! When the hero, having thrown off pursuit, sat down in view of the audience to devour with champing, smacking, voluptuous relish the deliciously browned pasteboard fowl he had stolen, the sympathetic children shared with him a primitive, restoring delight in food which was to add zest to their lives ever after.

It was soon over. Interludes of joy in the serious-minded gray of life are always short. It was increasingly short as the showman grew older and more asthmatic. He often looked very tired and always immeasurably ancient at the end, when he emerged from the black cloth, after Polichinelle had squeaked out his last thanks to the children for their sympathy and help, and he was often panting so that he leaned against the wall. But there was always a smile on his white face as he looked happily from one glowing child-face to another.

One of the bigger boys passed the hat around for the money every child had been saving in a corner of his desk, and the showman, after a bow, swept the few coppers into his pocket without looking at them. This was not through pride or decorum but because, compared to the children's applause, the money was of no consequence to him. What material needs, beyond a little food, an occasional bed, and enough ragged clothes to cover the skin, has one who, every day of his life, knows such satisfaction as his?

The children helped him pack up. One by one, the little figures of the comedies were rolled up in a ragged cloth, their battered wooden faces expressionless, their tinseled tawdry costumes threadbare, their stuffed arms and legs inert and limp, all quite unrecognizable as the sparkling personages of the plays. The bigger boys helped shut the box, unjointed the supports, strapped them on, and lifted the whole to the thin shoulders which stooped more and more under it as the years went on. The children cried out as he turned to leave the schoolhouse, "Good-by, Guignol! Good-by!" and the old tramp was off on his way to the next schoolhouse, miles away, perhaps over a mountain pass where snow still lingered on the road.

How many years he had thus walked in and out of colorless narrow lives with his color and drama no one knew, the old showman least of all, for he was quite unlettered, could not so much as write his name and did not know his numbers. But only the oldest people in the mountain villages could remember a time before he had lived in a little one-room shack on the outskirts of Urona, the "county town," and had varied his daily puppet-shows on a tiny stage there with these long tramps about the countryside. The children of Urona loved him as dearly as did the little mountaineers and watched as eagerly for his return from his pilgrimages. "Guignol is back!" they would announce prancingly to their mothers or nurses on seeing the old man pottering about his ramshackle little theater, or sitting in front of it on one of the low benches, eating the cornbread and onions which seemed to be his only food. The next day the audience assembled (no need to announce that there would be a performance), the mothers and nurses like giantesses on the diminutive benches set under the pollarded plane-trees of the boulevard.

Of course he had no license from the municipality thus to occupy a part of the best (indeed the only) show street of the impecunious little city. But all the members of the municipal council had, in their time,

sat on those low benches and screamed with delight
when Polichinelle double-crossed the policeman. They
no more thought of forbidding him to use their boulevard than of forbidding the sparrows which hopped
about him, living lives as bright as his, as unburdened
by possession and prosperity.

Indeed, as they came and went their anxious, responsible ways, the rulers of the community were as
little conscious of the old man's gray presence as of the
sparrows. Their eyes, clouded by successful calculations, were blind to the fact that the old showman was
every day thinner and grayer and more bent. He had
no one to think of him, and they had many other things
to occupy their important thoughts, charged as they
were with the welfare of the five thousand inhabitants
of Urona, trying to keep up the pavements and keep
down the beggars, to install sewers against the passionate protests of the older inhabitants, to hold their own
against the Préfet, to shore up the crumbling walls of
the twelfth-century church, to provide a monument to
the war dead as imposing as that of other towns of
their size—in general, to keep Urona sufficiently up
to the mark so that visiting Parisians would not find
too much to laugh at.

The historic storm of January, 1923, which, sweeping in from the Bay of Biscay, wrecked all the harbors along the Basque coast, tore on into the interior with frightful wind and rain such as the oldest inhabitants could not remember and laid low structures which had withstood the storms for centuries. From four o'clock one afternoon, when after a sudden blackness the wind burst upon the town, the tempest shrieked and yelled up and down the defenseless streets of Urona. Nobody ventured abroad, not even the dogs. Heavy wooden shutters were barred tight, and the people sitting within shuddered to hear the roaring of the river as it rose higher and higher, and the banging of the chimney-pots, scaffoldings, and street signs as the wind caught them and whirled them to destruction. At midnight the old stone bridge on the road to Spain went out with a crash, and in the same hour the enraged river, tearing its way over its embankments, flung huge blocks of stone from the ruined bridge up into the public square, where they lay for months thereafter.

But this marked the climax of the storm. By three o'clock the tempest had swept past, and when day broke the gray air lay still over the havoc wrought in the little city. The first calamity seen by the people who went cautiously out at dawn was that many of the beautiful plane-trees, the pride of the region, were shattered to splinters. And the first sounds they heard were the sobs of the old showman who stood in the midst of a mass of wreckage, weeping bitterly.

A great tree had crashed down on his flimsy little theater, crushing it and the benches. All night the rain had beaten down on those of his little figures which had not been pulverized by the fall of the tree. There was nothing left. Nothing. He stood there sobbing aloud, now and then with a cry stooping to pick up from the ruins the sodden corpse of one or another of his lifelong little friends and comrades.

The municipal council held an emergency meeting at the emergency hour of eight o'clock that morning to take measures for the relief of the town. And what do you think was the first action taken by those middle-aged, material-minded business men with bags under their eyes and waistcoats grossly distended? It was to vote money—town money—sacred tax-money—to build at once for Guignol a new theater and to stock it with as many marionettes as Paris could furnish that would fit the old showman's stories.

Yes, I know it sounds improbable. I can't help that.

Just as I set it down here, that is what really happened.

With half the roof torn from the Town Hall, with bricks from every chimney strewing the streets, with trees lying criss-cross on the boulevard, with the only bridge across the river gone, their first vote taken without a dissenting voice was for the old man weeping in the midst of his ruins—ruins which were theirs as well.

"He had the crocodile in his hands as I passed by— what was left of the crocodile," said the mayor, "all a shapeless mass of papier-mâché. Do you remember? The crocodile the gendarme backed into."

Did they remember!

"I saw something red on the ground off at one side," said the banker, "half trampled into the mud, and when I picked it up it was the red shirt of the miller. You know, the miller who fooled the devil."

"There lay the towers of Pampelune, splintered into matchwood," said the lawyer; "I could just make out what it had been. When I was a little boy, living in Gure Chocua, how grand those towers looked to me! No real castle has ever seemed half so fine.

"I left my little grandson crying his heart out because he had been told he would never see again the old soldier who had a wooden leg."

From the clouded eyes of those representative men, heavy with their success, looked out for an instant the clarity of little boys' eyes; for an instant the flabby flesh of their overfed bodies was gone, and they were little, lithe sprites racing down a country road in the morning of life, shouting, "Guignol! Guignol!"

Yes, the best that money could buy—they voted it with a will, and telegraphed the order to Paris that very morning.

In a week everything they could buy had arrived, and the old showman, his face gray, his head shaking in a beginning of palsy, but with his old smile quivering on his lips, was reverently handling such actors as he had never seen before, nor dreamed of. Real satin, heavy shimmering reds and blues, clad the fine ladies; real gold lace adorned the broadcloth of the gendarme's uniform; the old veteran's wooden leg was hooped with shining copper; and oh, Polichinelle! What a hump! What a glorious red nose! What silver lace upon his peaked cap! What marvelously fashioned hands with finger nails painted on fingers and thumbs! There was, it is true, no Roland, no miller, no countess. The old showman had drawn those stories from traditions too old for the great world to remember. But clever artisans of Urona were already working to reproduce the missing figures, and other nimble fingers were sewing on the costumes, every seam and button and fold of which was familiar to every one in town.

In a fortnight a new Guignol stood on the boulevard, superb in red paint picked out with gilt, and new rows of low benches stood before it. All day long the old showman hung about it, immaterial as a specter, but always with his tremulous smile—pulling on the cords running through patented arrangements of pulleys, so much better than anything he had ever had; or trying out the brightly painted scenery; or gloating over the finery of his actors.

When all was ready the gala performance was given. Marching down the boulevard, two by two, as on great fête days, shining silk hats on their bald heads, long-tailed frock coats on their corpulent bodies, the mayor with the broad red sash of his office girt about him, the *garde champêtre* in full uniform bringing up the rear, the municipal council arrived in a body and sat themselves down on the front benches, reserved for them as for the family of the bride at a wedding, with heavy tasseled cords. Behind them, thick as they could sit, were children and children and children—prettily dressed little girls and ragged little boys, small gentlemen in fawn-colored gaiters and plain little girls in worn black cotton dresses, the only thing in common between them the dewy brightness of their young eyes. Behind them, row upon row, standing up, were their fathers and their mothers and their grandfathers and their grandmothers, dressed in their best black as for Sunday mass, on their mature or withered faces a reflection from the light in the children's eyes.

Never was there such a show. When the curtain went up showing the familiar kitchen of the inn with the roast pasteboard fowl on the table, what a burst of applause! Such shouts of "Come in! Come in!" as at the little side door came the familiar knocking. As the door slowly, slowly opened, such expectant silence; and such enthusiasm when, thrust slyly around it, appeared the goggling eyes and great red impudent nose! *"Vive Polichinelle!"*

How eagerly they all called out the wrong directions to the pursuing gendarme as after the theft of the fowl he rushed about, trying to arrest the culprit! How magnificently did Polichinelle reward them with his great jovial bow and his shameless chuckle of joy!

The municipal council, sitting hunched on the low

benches, their great paunches resting on their knees, laughed over the old jokes and over their being there, till they wiped their eyes. But they remembered to fall respectfully silent during the pathetic scene of the countess and her lost son, so silent that one could hear the little girls sniffing and using their handkerchiefs.

The last show was "Polichinelle and the Crocodile," the latter brilliantly varnished and savagely toothed, so that the littler children shuddered as the gaping jaws opened wide. One little fellow called out as naïvely as the mountain children, "Look out! Look behind you! Take care!"—only to have the others say, "Sh! Sh!" and remind him in whispers that it was only the gendarme in danger.

The last act ended with Polichinelle's whirling dance of exultation in his own cunning and his thanks to the children for their help and sympathy. *"Vive Polichinelle! Vive Guignol!"* they cried as the curtain went down. And before they went back to the world of duty and responsibility and cause and effect, they lingered to laugh and chat as the collection was taken up, the wonderful collection, with bank bills and silver in it.

## "VIVE GUIGNOL!"

The next morning the old showman did not appear. When at noon they went to his little shed to look him up they found him dead on his ragged mattress, the white marble of his lips set in a smile.

I know it sounds melodramatic. But just as I tell it to you, so it happened. His heart had probably been weak for some time, the doctor said.

"Good-by, Guignol!"

# THE SAINT OF THE OLD SEMINARY

CHOOL was over for the day. The children's little hemp-soled *espadrilles* padded softly on the floor as they filed out before Mlle. Etchegaray. Her tired, keen, kind eyes looked at each one in turn. Well-dressed pale French children from bourgeois homes, with intelligent, irregular faces; Spanish children, ragged, dirty, Murillo-beautiful, their heads crusted with filth from the dens of the Old Seminary; dark little Basques carrying their heads high with pride in being Basque— Mlle. Etchegaray gave to each one the look that really sees. For twenty-five years parents in Mendiberria had counted on Mlle. Etchegaray's ability to see what was there—and to report it. Did some one say, "Isn't your Jeanne getting stoop-shouldered?" the first defensive answer of Jeanne's mother would be, "Why, Mlle. Etchegaray hasn't said anything to us about it!"

After the last bobbing dark head had vanished, the teacher looked toward the open door. She was seldom left to herself to straighten the things on her desk and go wearily up the stairs to her lodging. Juanito Tuán's father appeared. Not happy and elated as he should have been. Not in the least. Could something have gone wrong with that scholarship for Juanito? After all the trouble she had taken with the inspector to get it!

The Tuáns were Spanish, but old Enrique left off, today, all his usual formalities of greeting.

"He won't go," he announced tragically.

He evidently expected the teacher to know the reason without being told. She did.

With the hot-blooded lack of moderation which endeared her to the Basques and Spaniards of Mendiberria she said intensely, "I wish that Tomasina had choked to death on her mother's milk!"

64

Enrique Tuán's deeply lined swarthy face took for an instant an appeased look.

But Mlle. Etchegaray corrected herself conscientiously, characteristically: "No, I take that back. Tomasina is the only child I ever had in my classes whom I really couldn't endure. But that may be not as I think, because I can't stand posing and lying, but because she's so handsome and I'm ugly and old and a spinster. I don't wish she'd died, but I do wish to Heaven she would land her French sergeant, marry him, and have whatever it is she wants him for—leave off her mantilla, and wear hats, change her *espadrilles* for leather slippers, smoke cigarettes, be as French as she likes—only where we wouldn't have to see her— off in France somewhere." Mendiberria is in France, but Basques sometimes forget this.

Old Enrique, looking down at his blackened shoemaker's hands, said: "He'll never marry her. He's as ambitious as she. If only he could *get* his promotion and be stationed somewhere else along the frontier, and never show his face here again!"

"You mean—leave Tomasina for your Juanito? Tomasina for your daughter-in-law! You must be crazy! You know Tomasina!"

The old Spaniard fixed a somber gaze on her, his face working. In the silence she could hear his teeth grinding together.

"If Juanito wants her," he said finally, and leaned against the wall, wiping his forehead.

Emerging into the market-place, Mlle. Etchegaray turned toward the Tuán shop. Old Enrique sat at his bench, his hammer tapping fast, but the shop itself was empty. No customers sat on the brightly varnished benches which were the pride of the workman risen to proprietor; no foot pressed the strip of real carpet down the center; the pasteboard boxes of shoes on each side rose to the ceiling with no attendant to admire them. Mlle. Etchegaray knew where to look, across the square at the Martinez vegetable stand. A tall slender boy leaned against the door-jamb there, gazing at a girl in a brightly flowered dress who was bending over a display of cabbages and tomatoes and with pretty, sinuous, self-conscious gestures re-arranging them unnecessarily on the sloping boards of her stall. Old Enrique was watching them. His hands continued to tap blindly at the shoe he was re-soling, but his

66

blazing eyes cried, "Look out! Don't push me beyond what I can endure!"

She stepped close to his open window and proffered hastily all she had to give.

"I came down to have a talk with Juanito. I thought it might do some good to make him understand what a marvelous opportunity this scholarship is, what a wonderful life he would have as a doctor, what a shame it would be to miss—"

Young laughter rippled through the air. Tomasina and Juanito were standing close together now, looking into each other's eyes, laughing. The girl's black hair glistened in the sun. She turned at the waist, flexible and firm, and leaned to tease a parrot, brooding misanthropically on his perch. With a grating scream he pounced at her finger. But she drew it away with a flash and now, holding her hand high above her head, shook it at him tauntingly as if she had castanets between her fingers. Then, curving her white neck, she turned her eyes again on the boy. The magnetism of that glance could be felt all across the square.

Steps sounded, heavy, leather-soled French steps. Mlle. Etchegaray hastily looked another way, and moving forward, gazed through the dusty window of the chemist's shop at the familiar fly-specked bottles there. Presently she heard other steps behind her, not leather-soled, the soft scuff of *espadrilles*. Juanito walked slowly past, not seeing her. He passed his father without a glance and sank down in the shop on one of the grand new benches, gazing at his feet.

Young laughter rippled through the air. Tomasina and Sergeant Brugnol were standing close together, looking into each other's eyes and laughing. The girl's black hair glistened in the sun. She poured her personality into her eyes so that across the square it could be felt. But Sergeant Brugnol, though his fair face wore a dazzled expression, was evidently able to remind himself that he had other things to do than to chat with the market-gardener's daughter. Lingering and turning back after several starts to leave her, he finally, in spite of her animation, lifted his cap in the citified French way, scorned and envied by wearers of tight-fitting bérets, and went on down the street.

Tomasina's animation vanished. She watched him out of sight, her face dark and forbidding. The cobbler's hammer tapped away like an insistent, unwanted thought. When Mlle. Etchegaray went into the shop, Juanito looked up at her, startled, with so wan an ex-

pression of misery that she only asked for a pair of
shoestrings and went her way, passing, as she did so, a
group of tourists in their outlandish clothes. A guide
was talking to them in their outlandish language. A
good many tourists came to Mendiberria. Their guides
told them that Charlemagne—or was it Henry the
Fourth?—had done something or other there, in the
public square. Mendiberria people were of the opinion
that the auto-bus company invented this unlikely story
to get more trade.

Along with all the Basques and most of the Spanish
in town, Mlle. Etchegaray was indignant over the news
of the discovery by the French of the secret path used
by the Orthez smugglers and of the capture of their
whole convoy in the night. She was a functionary of
the French government, but she shared to the full the
opinion of her high-spirited race that no government
has a right to lay down a frontier across another people's territory. It was Basque on both sides, wasn't it?
A pity it would be if a Basque couldn't walk over the
mountain to his uncle and take him a twist of tobacco
without having the top of his head shot off by murderous frontier guards. Of course, the four Orthez brothers

did rather more than this, with their regular trips, loaded with bales of silks and tobacco and lace and what not; but their business was based on sound Basque principles. They were nice boys too, thought Mlle. Etchegaray, fidgeting restlessly about her quarters over the schoolroom—steady, decent young fellows, real Basques. It was a horror to think of their being taken off to a French prison.

Another stick in the fire of her wrath was that Sergeant Brugnol must be delighted. It is part of the system of guarding frontiers to have the guards and their officers always from a distant part of France. Sergeant Brugnol, a big-boned Fleming from near the Belgian frontier, would have said confidently that the black-haired, neatly made Southerners of Mendiberria were quite ignorant of him personally (all except that pretty little trick at the Martinez vegetable stand). But everybody in town knew that he was ambitious and joked about his burning desire to make a spectacular *coup* that would force his superiors to promote him. Mlle. Etchegaray walked to the window to see if the guards and their prisoners were visible yet in the road down from the mountain and turned away quickly lest she should see what she was looking for.

As for the traitor who had given him the information —at the thought, the school-teacher flung violently on the floor the book she chanced to have in her hand. A spy among them! It made her sick, as falsity always did. Who could it be? The Orthez boys had no enemies. She could imagine no one in Mendiberria capable of such treachery. The little shepherd boy who had run so fast down the mountain knew no more than that, as the Orthez band came along the path they always used, bent under their usual bales, suddenly the French frontier guards were all about them. From the pasture above he had heard men's voices shouting, scuffles on the stony path, Sergeant Brugnol's voice giving commands. He had run away then, all the way down to Mendiberria, knowing that certain people there would pay him well for a warning.

Mlle. Etchegaray decided that a violent counter-irritant was what she needed. Little Maria Benevente was once more out of school. There was nothing for it but to go down to the Old Seminary again to see what the matter was. She had been putting it off—not that she was a timid woman. Quite the contrary. But the Old Seminary! She was the only respectable woman in town who ever went near it. "Oh, well, in broad daylight they wouldn't cut anybody's throat," she reassured herself. And as for dirt and germs, they could be washed off. "I'll just spray my nose and throat with a disinfectant and go."

But she did not see the Old Seminary that day, nor think of it for many days to come. As she stepped out of the schoolhouse door she saw the men with their drawn faces, hurrying to tell her. A boy from an upland farm, running fleetly by short-cut paths, had brought into town the news that Juanito Tuán, the only child of old Enrique, the widower, had been with the Orthez boys, had resisted arrest, had attacked the officer in command, and had been shot dead. They were bringing his body down on a stretcher. Some one must go to tell his father, so that his first intimation of the catastrophe should not be Juanito's dead body with a bullet-hole through the temple.

Mlle. Etchegaray broke in on their agitated story with frantic exclamations of unbelief—"But Juanito had nothing to do with the Orthez boys! He never smuggled anything in his life! It *must* be a mistake!" The excited men cried her down with more of what the farm boy had reported; yes, yes, it was Juanito—his first trip, Juan Orthez had said; he had a bundle of

72

lace and silk on his back; he had seemed to go crazy when he saw the French officer, had leaped straight at the Sergeant; there was no possible doubt. Quick! She must go to tell old Enrique. Who else could do it? There was no other woman to whom the old cobbler ever spoke. He was a mad free-thinker who would drive Father Casimiro out of the house if he tried to go. Quick! The guards with their prisoners and Juanito's corpse might arrive at any moment. She still cried out that it was too dreadful, it could not be true. The men, waving their arms, urged her to be quick. Some of them were weeping with rage and sorrow. They all talked at once, motioning her to hurry.

The clamor of their voices rose so loud that a group of tourists, passing in an auto-bus, looked out and smiled to see how excitable Latins scream and gesticulate over nothing.

A few days after the funeral of Juanito Tuán, Mlle. Etchegaray, going down to see if there was anything she could do for his father, found the Tuán shop still tight closed. But as she stood an instant before it the door opened and Enrique motioned her to come in quickly. He shut the door behind her, and shaking one fist in the air, dragged her to a long crack in one of the shutters and bade her look. She saw, coming across the square toward them, like a picture of Youth Triumphant brilliantly painted by the sun, the blond officer of the frontier guard, the man who had shot Juanito dead, arm in arm with Tomasina Martinez in her best flowered silk. Her splendid eyes were flashing, her small head held proudly under a gala white lace mantilla. Smiling, looking deep into the other's blue eyes, her smooth scarlet lips moving in low intimate talk, she came closer and closer, unconscious of the fierce gaze upon her. They passed, brushing against the closed shutters. The murmur of their young voices came into the darkness like the hum of bees. They were gone.

Mlle. Etchegaray's first impulse was not to express her own astounded indignation at the sight of Tomasina flaunting on the arm of the man who had killed Juanito, but to quiet that of the infuriated old man beside her. She reminded him hastily that Tomasina, now she was grown up, was just what she had been as a child—a lying, cheating, play-acting little fraud, of too little account for decent people to bother with: "She is not worth even hating. She would have made

Juanito miserable. She will make this Frenchman miserable."

Old Enrique cut her short.

"She will make no man miserable any more," he said solemnly. Seeing the fear whitening the teacher's face, he said dryly, "No, I shall not need to touch her."

If she had known what he meant to do would she have tried to stop him? Why rack her brains about that? She was, in fact, the last person to know what he meant to do. The examination for the *certificats d'étude* approaching now, everything else dropped from her mind.

It was said in Mendiberria that during the last fortnight before those examinations Mlle. Etchegaray would not know if the house over her head were on fire. One after another, till late at night, she coached the children who were coming up. Everybody left her alone at such times, the honor of the town being involved. Sometimes mothers of the children with whom she was working came in silently to set down a covered dish of cooked food, but nobody stopped to gossip.

She had her usual success that year and emerged as

usual to find everything in her two-roomed lodging in disorder and the supplies in her tiny kitchen almost exhausted. Basket on arm, she went down to the marketplace. Enrique Tuán was working quietly at his bench, deftly splitting a thick piece of leather with his thin sharp leather-cutting knife. He was as gray as a corpse, lean and gaunt, but collected and self-possessed. As she passed he looked up at her and nodded, his eyes tired and old, quite emptied of their frenzy. She went across to buy some vegetables and found stout Mme. Martinez there, who waited on her silently, sighing heavily.

"Is Tomasina sick?" asked the school-teacher.

"*Non!* oh, *non*, Mademoiselle!" cried her mother, putting both hands up to cover her face and speaking in so strange a tone that Mlle. Etchegaray said no more.

She usually stood on her professional dignity and waited till people told her local news of their own accord, but now she hurried into the bakeshop and asked the baker, point-blank, "Why isn't Tomasina at the Martinez stall?"

"She knows better than to show her face where we can see it," said the baker, folding his arms over his apron. And then, seeing her blankness, "Why, Mlle. Etchegaray, hadn't you *heard?*"

No, she had heard nothing, she told him impatiently; he knew as well as she that it was the time of final examinations.

"Well, Enrique Tuán found in the rubbish heap back of their home a letter, half torn up, of Tomasina's to Juanito. *She'd* been the one to put him up to joining the Orthez boys. *She* made him do it! To get some lace and truck for her, she told him. But it really was so she could find from him which path they used, and when they'd be coming on it, and then she ran to tell Sergeant Brugnol, to get a stand-in with him." Seeing incredulity mingled with the shock on the school-teacher's face, he went on, "Enrique's been showing the letter around. Everybody's seen it. It's all written out plain, her teasing and tormenting Juanito till he said he'd make just one trip. Her father doesn't deny it. The dirty ——!" He spat, wiped his mouth with his hand, and went on: "Enrique got the Sergeant's old housekeeper to let him and some others see the map the Sergeant used the night of the capture. The place and the hour were written on the margin—in Tomasina's handwriting, the same as in the letter. And he found out that late that night, just before the guards started up the mountain, she—"

"Never mind the rest," said the school-teacher, faintly. She was literally cold at the recollection of Tomasina as she had last seen her, triumphant on the arm of . . .

The baker was thinking of that too. He went on: "The first day after Enrique had told all this, she tried to come to the café with her Frenchman, dressed up the way she had been ever since, with her silk dress and leather slippers and white mantilla. It wasn't so white by the time she got out. We men did no more than turn our backs on them. But the boys, Juanito's friends, had rotten eggs in their pockets. She hasn't been seen out of the house since."

"She can't stay in the house the rest of her life," said Mlle. Etchegaray.

"She might go jump off the cliff on Izcohébie hill then," suggested the baker, changing the position of some rolls on his counter.

"Does the French Sergeant go to see her?"

"No, he's got his promotion and gone. But he'd dropped her before that, as soon as he heard how she got her information. Even frontier guards have *some*

78

limits! She's done for herself this time, Tomasina has. She's caught where not even she can find a way out."

II

If Mlle. Etchegaray had been the last to learn that Tomasina had done for herself, she was the first to know of the way out which Tomasina had found.

When she came back in the autumn after the two months of the summer vacation, she brought with her an old cousin from her home village to help her get through the rush of the first two weeks. Cousin Anna did the marketing, and so Mlle. Etchegaray, never going down to *la place*, heard no more about Tomasina than from the babble of the children who told her that twice during the summer the girl had tried to return to her work on the square, "but a half an hour of what she got there sent her back to the house." Her father's hair was quite white. Her mother wept if any one spoke to her. The neighbors said that Tomasina had been like a wild cat at first: everybody on the street could hear her screaming at her parents. But since her last sortie there had been absolute silence. "Maybe she's dead," said one child hopefully, catching his ball neatly.

Little Maria Benevente was again not in school.

"I'd better go to look her up while Cousin Anna is here," thought Mlle. Etchegaray. "It's all very well not to be timid. But when a person has to make a visit to the Old Seminary, two are better than one."

As they went down the muddy, rutted lane, Cousin Anna asked, "I never happened to hear why they call that frightful old tenement-house the 'Old Seminary.'"

"Because it is. It had been a seminary, crammed with boys learning how to be priests, from I don't know what date up to the time of the separation of church and state. Then of course the church had to vacate it."

"*Oh!*" said Cousin Anna, who was a good Clerical. "What a shame!"

"Guess again!" said the school-teacher, stepping wide to avoid a pile of filth. "It was the best piece of good luck they ever had. All the sympathizers with the church, oppressed by the wicked government, turned their purses inside out. Money just poured in —from as far as South America, a lot of it. They built themselves the New Seminary. You know it, that splendid big *château* on the West Road. Bathrooms they have now, and steam heat and hot and cold water and a hand-ball court of their own. They owe a vote of thanks to the government for getting them out of the medieval rookery where they'd been. Nothing succeeds like being oppressed."

Cousin Anna looked her disapproval, sternly. Presently she said: "But I don't see what call the Municipal Council had, even if they are godless, for letting the Old Seminary fall into such frightful neglect."

Mlle. Etchegaray laughed grimly: "It wasn't the godless party that managed that! The council wanted to put it in good shape to rent to poor families. But somehow a rumor got abroad that things would be made hot for any daughter of the church who let her husband vote to put to secular uses a building that had belonged to ecclesiastics. And most of the wives of the council are very devout. So the council just never could get a majority to vote to use it for lodgings for the poor of the town. They preferred to let it stand idle, unguarded, open to the weather, doors unlocked, plundered of everything that could be torn loose. And little by little—I hope they're rejoiced to see it—it's been lived in by riff-raff, toughs, bums, most of them Spanish, drifted over the frontier because Spain was too hot for them. By and by they began to bring their women-folks. You can imagine what they were like. It's their children I have at school."

Cousin Anna interrupted her here by an exclamation: "Heavens! What's that horrible smell!" She buried her nose in her handkerchief.

"The Old Seminary," said Mlle. Etchegaray, fiercely. "A good many of the children in my class live in that smell and bring it with them when they come to school."

They were at the entrance and turned in now between tall, battered stone posts which had once been handsomely carved. From them hung a few splinters of what had been gates. The two women had been seen, and from out the long, leprous, tumbledown building before them a crowd of children poured out to meet them. "Mademoiselle! Mademoiselle!" they shrieked, enchanted to see the revered ruler of the classroom come visiting. Around them eddied gusts of the fetid odor of sweaty, unwashed, excreting human beings, moldy rags, and decayed refuse.

Mlle. Etchegaray said heatedly in Basque to her horrified old cousin, "Don't you dare show a thing of what you're feeling. And take that handkerchief down from your nose this instant!"

The children were all about them now, many even

of the little ones drooping under baby brothers and sisters, all of them, babies and children alike, indistinguishably filthy, ragged, their heads matted with eczema sores, their hands and legs and feet and faces crusted with dirt and scabs of mange, their finger nails like black claws, their smiling lips and soft, brilliant eyes lovely as those of cherubim. Mlle. Etchegaray's heart, as so many times before, dissolved in a wild, indignant tenderness. She looked more grenadier-like than before. But the children knew her. They caught at her hands; they looked at her adoringly.

"I've come to see Maria Benevente," she said.

"The Beneventes live in the stable now," they cried, proud to be guides. "We will show you. And her mother had another baby just now."

The procession moved across the foul, garbage-strewn paving-stones of the courtyard, under the eyes of sluttish black-haired women and rowdy-looking men dressed in grimy rags, leaning out of holes which had been window-frames before the woodwork of the house had been torn out to make cooking-fires.

"Here's where the Beneventes live," said the children, stopping before what looked like the entrance to a vegetable cellar.

Cousin Anna gasped and stepped back, but Mlle. Etchegaray drew her firmly into the blackness. They found themselves standing on an earthen floor at one end of a long, narrow shed. At the far end a square hole in the stone wall let in rays of daylight that slanted down upon a woman lying on a mattress, the small round head of a tiny baby tucked into the crook of her arm. The same light showed, kneeling before a large wooden trough set on the ground, a woman washing clothes. The swish of the water as she lifted a cloth from it came to their ears. Hearing some one enter, she turned her head to peer into the dark, wringing out the cloth as she did so. Something about the gesture, very free, very graceful, was familiar to Mlle. Etchegaray. She took a long step forward as if to see and stopped short with a smothered exclamation.

The other drew her hands quietly from the soapy water, rose to her feet, and wiping her hands on her apron with a servant's gesture, came forward, her large dark eyes fixed intently on the school-teacher's.

"Yes, Mlle. Etchegaray, it is Tomasina," she said in a humble, earnest voice. "God has been very good to me. Just when I thought the burden of my sin more than I could bear, He sent the blessed St. Teresa to me to show me how to expiate it. She told me to leave behind my great misery and led me here. I saw her stand—glorious!—in the courtyard here, beckoning me in."

"I'd have died without her this morning, and the baby too," said the woman from the bed. "See how clean she has made everything. Isn't it beautiful?" She put her hand on the coarse white sheet which covered her.

Tomasina stood before Mlle. Etchegaray, her eyes dropped, her hands, reddened and swollen by washing, put together on her breast in the attitude of prayer. She was dressed like the poorest, in cheap black cotton, with an apron of coarse gray stuff. Her hair was hidden under a black cotton kerchief drawn tightly around her head.

Mlle. Etchegaray looked at her in a stunned silence.

Cousin Anna's heart was outraged by such unresponsiveness. "I don't know what you've done that's wrong," she said warmly, laying her hand on Tomasina's shoulder, "but I'm sure it is glorious to do what you are doing now."

Tomasina's heavy white eyelids fluttered. She murmured, "God has been good to me, a sinner," but she did not look up.

Mlle. Etchegaray, gazing at her in the twilight, still said nothing.

She kept the same silence before the flurry of talk that ran around town as the news spread. Everybody else exclaimed and speculated, but Mlle. Etchegaray made no comments save by the shrugged shoulders and widespread hands of professed ignorance.

At first everybody echoed Enrique's contemptuous comments, "What's the girl up to *now?*"

"It's just another of her tricks. She'll soon get tired of it."

"Wouldn't it make you laugh to think of Tomasina Martinez being .visited by the saints!" (The story of her vision was soon well known.) "Somebody in Heaven must have given St. Teresa the wrong address."

"Father Casimiro isn't any too enthusiastic, I hear. He asked her why she didn't go into a convent. She says she told him she needed a much harder penance. That's *one* way to put it! You couldn't get her into a convent! She wants to be the whole thing wherever she is!"

But as months went on, another note began to sound. People began to protest against Enrique's implacable bitterness.

"After all, Enrique, what more could anybody do for a penance? Nobody scrubs floors and washes children's heads and lays out the dead and takes care of old women with cancer just to show off. That's not playacting!"

"You're playing audience for her this minute!" said Enrique sourly.

Later: "She has put a statue of St. Teresa up in a shrine on the wall of the courtyard just where she saw her vision. And after each piece of her work she goes out there to pray, rain or shine, kneeling on the paving-stone."

"Where she can be seen," said Enrique.

Mlle. Etchegaray never commented on such reports, but now she asked, "Where did she get a statue? I thought Father Casimiro didn't—"

"Oh, she doesn't have Father Casimiro for her confessor any more! She gets up at four o'clock in the morning and walks clear down the valley to St. Pé, to the priest there. He gave her the statue."

The next time she met Father Casimiro on the street

Mlle. Etchegaray surprised the mild, absent-minded old priest by stopping to shake hands with him and in the most cordial manner to pass the time of day. He was not used to such friendliness from one of the anti-clericals.

The tone of the general talk in town became more and more respectful: "Those people in the Old Seminary seem to think a great deal of Tomasina. They get her in to settle their quarrels, it seems, and have her take care of their money—the better ones, that is, with families. Some of the tough men use terrible language to her, they say. She never answers a word, just stops whatever work she is doing, puts her hands together on her breast, and begins to pray. Some of them were drunk the other day, I hear, and when she started to sweep the courtyard they began to yell foul words at her. She knelt down to pray for them, and one of them struck her over the head with his stick. They say when she fell the women burst out of the house, dozens of them, screaming like tigresses, and landed on the men as if they'd tear their eyes out. There was a free-for-all fight, about ten women to every man, and the men drunk. They ended by making the fellow who had struck her come to ask her pardon. But she wouldn't let him, took him out before St. Teresa's shrine, and bade him make his excuses there, on his knees, to the saint. She's had her head tied up ever since."

"She thinks a bandage looks like a halo," growled Enrique.

The winter wore on, and one day a mother bringing a child to school stopped to tell Mlle. Etchegaray of a dramatic happening that was in everybody's talk: "A couple of drunks from the Old Seminary got to fighting with knives in the marketplace yesterday, and one of the children ran quick to get Tomasina. The moment the fighters saw her come up to them they stopped and looked foolish and went off, different ways. It was the first time she's been out on the street there since—you know when. Her face was as *white*—! they say, and shining! Like a lighted window, somebody told me. People stood back to let her pass, and some of the Frenchmen took off their hats. She didn't look at a soul, kept her head bent over her clasped hands, praying all the time."

"Did Enrique Tuán see her?" asked Mlle. Etchegaray.

"Yes, she passed just in front of his shop. He looked at her like a demon. People didn't like it. It's about time he stopped saying those awful things about her anyhow. It's not Christian to keep up your grievance so long. The people down at St. Pé are all talking about her. Their priest says she is wonderful. They think it very queer, the people in her own town not appreciating her more."

Later: "Who do you think came today to our doors, begging, with a basket on her back, but Tomasina Martinez! She was begging for food and clothes for a poor family. My husband said, 'Tomasina! You begging!' She answered in a little voice as clear as a bird's, 'God is good to me a sinner, to let me serve his poor.' Our Jeannot—you know what a tender-hearted little fellow he is—burst out crying and ran after her to ask her blessing."

She came thus to Mlle. Etchegaray's door, begging for her poor. Mlle. Etchegaray had always, ever since she had been in Mendiberria, given everything she could possibly spare, food, clothing, and money, to these of her school children who came from the Old Seminary. But she did not tell Tomasina this. After a moment's hesitation she said soberly she would see what she could do and went off to ransack the shelves of her tiny pantry. Tomasina, left alone, did not stir from where she stood in the middle of the floor. She bent her black coifed head over her clasped hands and began to pray.

Mlle. Etchegaray, coming back, saw this picturesque tableau of piety and was unexpectedly set upon by an emotion which translated itself—before she could restrain it—into a small smile. Tomasina opened her eyes, caught the smile on the school-teacher's lips. She closed her eyes more tightly and raised her prayers to a murmur. She never went again to the schoolhouse to beg.

But Juanito Tuán's father came. As spring approached and doors were opened, he sat many times of an evening on the doorstep of the schoolhouse, talking half to the school-teacher, correcting arithmetic papers back of him, and half to the blackness before him.

"She is a devil, that girl, simply a devil. It must be Satan himself who tells her how to fool people. First she killed Juanito, and now she makes everybody forget him. Nobody but his poor old father remembers him, and what have I done? I am the one who has pushed her up to where she always wanted to be. My son is dead and done for, and his friends taking off their hats to the woman who killed him. This business of begging now—that she's invented to keep people thinking about her—I see them, man after man, stepping back to let her pass. And the municipal council giving in to her, when they never would even let you put the case to them!" (Tomasina had suddenly appeared before the council, and speaking with such sweetness and devotion about her poor that even the most skeptical were moved, had prevailed on them to clean and repair the Old Seminary.) "Is Juanito any less dead because she puts on all these airs? He lies moldering in his grave, and his father has put his murderess where she gets what she wants. I did it! I!"

Sometimes the tired teacher, bending over the same mistakes in subtraction which she had corrected for a quarter of a century, heard him run wildly down the path in the darkness, weeping and crying, "I did it! I! I!"

But the next evening she would hear his voice again from the doorstep, moaning: "She says she is happy! That false, murdering woman says she is happier now than ever in her life. People who won't let me so much as say Juanito's name to them tell me: 'Look at her face as she goes along praying. Isn't that a beautiful happiness on it?' How did she get that happiness they all admire? By killing my boy. Yes, it was a fine thing for her and her soul when she killed Juanito. He lies in his grave so that she can be happy. 'Perhaps,' I tell people, 'you would like to have her murder *your* boy, so that she could repent even more gloriously.' "

Sometimes he interrupted his dreary muttering to call back: "Mademoiselle, *you* know, don't you, that all this saint business is just because there wasn't any other way she could get out of her hole?" She took these questions as part of his monologue and did not answer, but once he got up and came into the lighted schoolroom, his blood-shot eyes blank with their long gaze into darkness, his gray hair shaggy with neglect, the dirt deep in the creases of his swarthy face, which he no longer remembered to wash. "See here!" he said challengingly. "You know as well as I, don't you, that all this is no more than just another way—the only way she had left—for Tomasina to go on being Tomasina?"

At first the gaunt school-teacher only lifted her eyebrows and shoulders and spread out her hands in the gesture of professed ignorance. When she spoke, it was slowly, with long spaces between her three words: "I don't know," she said.

93

People began coming up from the village of St. Pé to pray for special favors before the St. Teresa of the Old Seminary and to ask Tomasina to pray with them. One woman had left her little girl very sick with a sore throat to come up to ask Tomasina to pray for her. At the very hour—so the story went around—that Tomasina left the floor she was scrubbing and went down on her knees on the stones of the courtyard, the little girl in St. Pé smiled, said, "Oh, Grandmère, I feel so much better!" and when the mother reached home the fever had gone and the child was almost well.

"I know which book of pious stories that comes out of," growled Enrique. "It had a blue cover. That was the third story in it. I had it read to me when I was a boy, and so had she."

But fewer and fewer people would listen to Enrique. He might at least, they thought, not say such things to people who had come from another town all the way to a shrine in Mendiberria. They murmured, too, at Father Casimiro's passive, ungracious attitude. It was because he was getting old, they said. A younger priest would have helped Tomasina more, would have appreciated her, as the priest of St. Pé did. One day an auto-bus-load of pilgrim excursionists drove all the way around from Lourdes, addressed themselves (naturally) to the priest of the parish, and said they would like to see the holy woman of whom they had heard and to pray with her before her shrine. Father Casimiro told them that he had not one but many holy women in his parish, and that he thought holiness was best practiced without too many spectators. And sent them away. Only think what a priest like the one at St. Pé would have done with such an opening!

The next autumn, when Mlle. Etchegaray came back once more from her two months' vacation, she found the Tuán shop shut. Enrique paid so little attention to his work now, she heard, that people didn't give the cantankerous old man their custom. He scarcely seemed to notice whether he had work or not, going aimlessly up and down the streets as if he were looking for some one, sitting by Juanito's grave, his hand laid on it, and standing opposite the entrance to the Old Seminary, watching Tomasina.

Here for a time he was, by gusts, violent and abusive, calling out such jibes as "Tomasina! Tomasina! Why do you always choose the two times when the men are coming and going to work to be out sweeping the courtyard?" or accosting visitors with the suggestion that they go to Father Casimiro for an account of what was happening at the Old Seminary: "After all, *he* is the priest of this parish!" Or he shouted, the tears running down his cheeks, "Juanito! Juanito! Ask her who Juanito was!" Tomasina had once suddenly crossed the road, knelt in the mud before the dirty old man, and folding her hands in the gesture of prayer, her lovely face shining with the white fire of exaltation, said gently and humbly to him, "Punish me as you wish. It will be what I deserve." The old man had broken from his tears into dreadful laughter then, and looking from her to the deeply moved group of pilgrims back of her, cried out, "Always where there's somebody to see, my girl!"

But he had been made to understand not too gently by the authorities of the town that this sort of rowdyism would not be permitted. After this he stood silent, skeleton-thin and ragged, the incarnation of dirt and misery, tears running down his cheeks as though from a never-exhausted reservoir. When his half-starved old body could endure no more he shuffled back to Juanito's grave and sat beside it, resting, his hand laid across it as though to try to reach his son. And when he could stand again, he returned to his place across the road from

Tomasina. Sometimes one of the many visitors to the shrine of the Old Seminary saw him standing thus, forlorn and emaciated, took him for a beggar, and offered him alms. Never more than once!

He seemed not to take his eyes from Tomasina. He saw her followed by adoring children, transformed by the cleanliness and care she gave them, kneeling with them before the statue of St. Teresa like their young spiritual mother; he saw her sweetly teaching the same children to play without the Stone Age ferocity that had been their habit; he saw the men and women in the tenement, lifted from their misery of poverty by the gifts of pilgrims to their shrine, consult and obey her; he saw many of the expressive, emotional Spanish women kneel to kiss her hand, although she always drew back with a pained look and motioned them to St. Teresa; he saw people coming to pray beside her, not only from St. Pé and the villages down the valley and beyond, but her own townspeople, women who had known and loved Juanito as a little boy, but who now, pale and anxious, thought of nothing but the sick person for whom they were praying. Exhausted, he went to sit by Juanito's grave and returned to see the young priest from St. Pé with a visiting priest come to look into Tomasina's story and listen to the girl, kneeling before the shrine, describe once more the vision that had brought her there. He saw an auto-bus of pilgrims from Lourdes, this time not consulting Father Casimiro, stop at the entrance of the lane and discharge a crowd of visitors who, after praying at the shrine, left Tomasina's hands full of offerings of which she kept not a penny for herself. He saw finally, one day, a delegation of students file into the courtyard and kneel before the shrine. Afterward the priest who was their leader asked Tomasina with deference if she could tell them of her vision. Old Enrique saw her leave the huge pan of potatoes she was peeling and come humbly forward, wiping her stained hands on her apron, her beautiful face like alabaster under the severe folds of her black headkerchief. He saw her listeners absorbed, transported, their sensitive young lips parted. They were of Juanito's age at the time of his death, as big as men, as simple-hearted as boys. He saw Tomasina's eyelids raised once, only once, and saw her young audience thrill to the magnetism of her great eyes, deep with emotion.

After they went away, he walked steadily across the street and into the courtyard, drawing out his long leather-cutting knife, and without a word, without a change of expression on his sad old face, stabbed Tomasina to the heart.

### III

Mlle. Etchegaray was leaving Mendiberria. Not for the summer. For always. The day after Father Casimiro had departed for his new parish far up in the mountains, she had put in her application to be transferred to another school. She had gone to see the old priest off at the station, a great bouquet of flowers for him in her unbeliever's hand, and had, amazingly, asked him for his blessing. He had shown no surprise at this. He was perhaps too much broken by the shock of his transfer to a strange parish to have vitality enough left to be surprised at anything.

The day she was to leave town, Mlle. Etchegaray set out on the road to the Old Seminary. It was marked from afar by a cloud of sun-gilded dust which hung quivering over the crowd like dust at a fair. Like a fair it was lined with booths, selling souvenirs. Behind the booths were people she knew, old students of hers, very animated and active now, as they counted out change and called attention, leaning over their counters,

to the attractions of their wares. Many of the booths
were selling eatables too, for the crowds of pilgrims
needed to be fed. She saw the baker bustling about,
setting out hundreds of rolls, fresh from the oven. His
was one of the largest and finest of the booths.

As she came nearer the building the movement of the
crowd became slower. They inched themselves forward
a little at a time and stood for long periods without
advancing at all. Visitors were being admitted to the
courtyard by groups of forty at a time. Up and down
the waiting line moved vendors of souvenirs on foot,
some selling relics, although that was forbidden by
both the church and the municipal authorities. "A
piece of wood from the broom used by the martyr the
day of her death," a woman would say, drawing her
relic furtively from under her shawl and speaking in a
low voice; "guaranteed authentic." Every one now
crowded to one side to allow an excited group to pass,
returning from the shrine. The news flew about, per-
vasive as the dust: "A cure! That woman in the middle
hadn't walked for ten years!" Some well-tailored
North American women with loud voices laughed and
called back and forth to each other as they took snap-
shots.

A smartly dressed young man fought his way down the line, asking, "Which is Mlle. Etchegaray? I was told the school-teacher was here." When he reached her he said, speaking in her ear in a furtive tone like that of the vendors of relics, that he was a reporter from a Socialist newspaper in Paris, sent down to make an investigation, and to report along modern scientific lines on all this furore. He looked at her knowingly, with a smile of secret understanding. "I've been told that you—a highly intelligent, thinking person—can give me the real inside facts of the matter, and I'd like to make an appointment to get some stuff from you that will—"

"I can tell you the facts right here," said Mlle. Etchegaray, breaking in on his whispering with her natural tone. "A girl of this town who had done a great wrong gave the rest of her life to self-inflicted penance for it, devoting herself to the poorest miserables, from whom the rest of us held aloof. She served them to the hour of her death, and since then has been serving them and all other poor by her example, which has caused the founding of a national organization of girls of good family to give part of their superfluities and time to the needy. She was killed by an insane man who died in prison shortly after. There have been many authentic cures made on the place where she died, and people love her memory for them. She has brought much prosperity to her townspeople, as you can see for yourself. The former priest of the parish was too old and too infirm to take charge of the complex situation always caused by a sudden influx of pilgrims, and has been sent to a smaller parish more within his powers. Those are the facts, if facts are what you are looking for." She added conscientiously, "I have forgotten to say that she was very beautiful."

"But—but—" The smart young man was disconcerted. "I was told that you knew all about—"

Mlle. Etchegaray lifted her shoulders and spread out her hands. "I know nothing whatever about anything," she told him, passing forward with the crowd into the courtyard.

When she came out, half an hour later, she turned away from the crowd, off into the waste country covered by gorse, its thorny, graceless branches hung with yellow bloom. She walked a long time there, following aimlessly one after another of the wandering sheeptracks through it, her head sometimes bent, sometimes lifted to look up at the mountain where Juanito was killed, sometimes turned to look back at the Old Seminary. Presently, picking a few of the harsh, spiky sprays of blossoming gorse, she went to lay them on the neglected, unmarked grave of old Enrique.

## AN ANCESTRAL HOME

 DON'T know, of course, who teaches French in the High School of your town; but if yours is an average big-village, small-town community, I can make a guess at what she is like—one of those hard-working wheel-horses of the American public-school system, who can be counted on, year after year, no matter what sort of student material she receives, to turn out a creditable number of passed examinations. Probably she wears pince-nez glasses on a well-shaped nose, can recite any rule in the French grammar, and when she pronounces French has an

American accent, which could, as the phrase goes, be sliced with a knife and spread on like cheese. If so, you can make a good mental picture of Miss Mary Haven Palmer.

As you watch the teacher in your town walking soberly from her boarding-house to the High School and back, always on time, her winter feet in overshoes, her November and April feet in rubbers, her October and May ones in low-heeled black Oxfords, you probably think, just as Millersburg people thought of Miss Palmer, "There goes a reliable woman" (meaning by "reliable" what people usually mean—somebody who has suppressed, if she ever had it, a living personality). Well, you're probably wrong. At least the people in Millersburg were wrong. For in this land of ours (always from the very first a melting-pot) every American, even the most overshoed and resigned, has one door imaginatively open to the unknown and the uncertain. Your teacher probably has what we all have, at least one queer ancestor, different from the Spencers and Perkinses and Randolphs and Smiths whose predictable qualities mostly rule our lives. Haven't you heard perfectly "reliable" account-keepers and real-estate agents speak with wistful pride of a French, or

Irish, or Highland Scotch grandmother, of a streak of wild Cornish, or Bohemian, or Welch, or even American Indian blood? In Miss Palmer's case the element which lightened the relentless reliability of the Havens and Palmers and Websters of her ancestry was a mystery. For seventy-seven years there had been in her family two letters addressed to one of her great-grandfathers, written in an unknown language. I mean, *unknown.*

They were nothing much to look at, the two yellowed, old, clumsily hand-made envelopes with the great-grandfather's name (John Daran) very oddly foreignized to Juanech Daranatz. The family tradition amounted to no more than that when back in the early '50's the first letter came to the town of Oxford Mills, Maine, where John Daran and his wife Phebe Webster then lived, their great-grandfather had claimed it from the puzzled postmaster. But he died shortly after, and when the next letter arrived there was no one to read it. There was no way to know to whom to return it, either, since like the first it came from some country which had as yet, in the 1850's, no postage stamps, and whatever was written on the outside was as unintelligible as the letters themselves. Phebe, left a penniless young widow with three little girls, had naturally married again, this time one Elmer Sackett. She had died young too, leaving her three little Darans to be brought up and married off by the Sacketts, who had moved back to where they really belonged, inland in Massachusetts. They had never had any interest, of course, in Phebe's first husband in Maine and handed down no more than a rumor that he had been a sailor-man in his youth. He left behind him nothing but the two letters, full of clearly written but preposterous words like "eztakizut," "gure," "ukan," "bederatzi," and "zaldiak." But in them he provided food for the imagination of his descendants. The matter-of-fact and the commonplace could never quite get the Webster and Palmer shoulders to the mat as long as those strange missives continued, from the various bureau-drawers in which they were kept, to radiate creative mystery.

For nearly eighty years they had provided dream-stuff for the younger members of those respectable New England families when, on the death of an aunt, they came to Miss Mary Palmer. Before she put them away in her bureau-drawer she showed them to the people in her boarding-house, who said, as everybody else had, that they were "real curiosities." Her own comment on them as she took them back was one befitting a self-respecting Palmer whose middle name was Haven: "Probably nothing more than dunning letters about a bill my sailor great-grandfather left behind him in a foreign port."

But that was not at all the way she thought of them. She might look reliable and answer your "Pleasant day" with the expected "Rather warm for this time of year," but as like as not, even as she spoke she was reveling in Romance—the letters were perhaps, that day, from a beautiful sweetheart her great-grandfather had left behind him in Peru—another time they were from a fellow pirate, threatening exposure if money was not sent—they were from a rich old Chinese merchant longing to reward the American sailor who had saved his life at sea—they were from a—whatever else they were, they always opened a road out of the Millersburg High School and her boarding-house, where everything was settled beforehand, into a world where anything might happen.

Then one day something did. The clew which had been withheld so long came as the reward of a habit of Miss Palmer's as unusual as meritorious. She was that rare person who practices what everybody preaches, the daily use of dictionary and encyclopedia. When tennis produced a player spoken of as a Basque, she, like everybody else in These States, did not know what a Basque was. But unlike anybody else, she took down Volume Balt-Brai of the encyclopedia. Her practiced school-teacher fingers were turning over the pages, her eyes wandering from "Basket-ball" to "Basle" to "Basoche," when, out of the familiar words, one sprang up at her with a shout. One of *her* words! One of those that had lain so long on the pages of her great-grandfather's letters! The word "bederatzi."

Before she even rightly knew what she had seen, her hands had begun to tremble. She could hardly find her place on the page again, because of the knocking of her heart. Yes, there it was, in the article on the Basque language. It was translated as meaning "ten." It was, then, a real word, in a real language.

Miss Palmer's eyes raced down the page, reading wild snatches: "—has absolutely no connection with any other known human language—origin, like that of the Basque people, total mystery—no one not a Basque has ever learned it—only theory occasionally advanced by a few scholars is that Basques may be descendants of the picture-painting cavemen of the Stone Age—only Stone Age words in language—never—" She skipped whole paragraphs, looking wildly for another of "her" words. Another would be a proof. And fell headlong over another: "zaldiak." It meant "the horses."

So now she guessed—she knew! Her great-grandfather was not John Daran, a Yankee sailor who had stopped in a foreign port, but Juanech Daranatz, a Basque, who—perhaps for the love of Phebe Webster—had settled in a Yankee port. She had Basque blood—she, Mary Haven Palmer, who never till then had heard of such a people.

II

The smart, tailored, perfumed lawyer at Biarritz saw at a glance that the two old letters brought him by the foreign lady were dated from Yende-Onak. That was enough for him. "Some picayune inheritance quarrel about who's going to have the cow-shed," he thought, handing them back to her, and explaining that the person to take her case was M. Etcheberry, up in St. Jean Pied-de-Port. "The old gentleman has been there for a century or so," he said playfully, "and is related to nearly everybody in that valley." He escorted her to the door, bowing low and saying, "At your service always, Madame," and thinking, "Let old Etcheberry settle who gets the extra franc and have a penny for his pains."

As old M. Etcheberry, gray and shabby in his musty-smelling office at St. Jean Pied-de-Port, held out his hand for the letters, his eye ran appraisingly over his unexpected client. Queer—in spite of her ungraceful foreign stiffness and ugly French-looking hat and ridiculous leather shoes, she reminded him of some one. She looked agitated, he noticed, and was breathing very quickly. Perhaps she had, like his old wife, a troublesome heart. Perhaps just emotional. Before beginning to read her letters he glanced at his shelves to make sure the bottle of smelling-salts was there.

When he finished he laid the letters down and put the tips of his fingers together. "I'm afraid the title would be hard to establish. The matter has been allowed to run rather a long—"

"What! What matter?" cried the foreign lady with an explosive wildness out of keeping with her looks. She added, "*I* don't know what's *in* those letters."

The lawyer was startled. Shocked. In these days of

public schools! A woman who wore eye-glasses. "Can't you *read?*" he asked, astonished.

"Not Basque," she admitted.

He swallowed, and taking up the letters, began to translate them into French.

It was naturally rather a long and involved explanation, since it required considerable ransacking of old papers and rather a complete genealogy of that branch of the Daranatz family that lived in Yende-Onak. "Your great-grandfather Juan must have left Gure Chocua about 1850," he surmised. "This letter of '53—"

"Gooray Chokeyouah?" asked his visitor, puzzled, and pronouncing the strange syllables with an effort. "I thought you told me the village was called Yende-Onak."

"Oh, Gure Chocua is the name of the Daranatz farm," explained the lawyer; "that is, it's not an uncommon name for Basque homes. It only means 'our home' or 'our corner.'" He smiled a little, secretly; added, "Almost, really 'our hole,'" and went on, "Your great-grandfather had a claim to half the Daranatz inheritance, such as it was, the only other heir being his little sister, then six years old, as I see from this statement sworn to before my father, when no news came from America. That sister must be Aunt Maï. Just let me look at the dates. Yes, it is. She's living at Gure Chocua now. Almost the only one of your family left. Her daughter married a Daranatz cousin from St. Jean Pied-de-Port here and had one son, Gratien. But both husband and wife died when Gratien was still a baby. Aunt Maï brought him up. He is married now, too."

His visitor had been opening and shutting her mouth as if trying to speak and now when he paused broke out, "But—but—do you mean to say my great-grandfather's sister is still *living!*"

The old man was nettled. "You speak as though seventy-seven years were seventy-seven centuries. Aunt Maï isn't a day over eighty-three. She's vigorous as you are." In his mind he added, "She could walk *your* legs off, any day." And went on aloud, "I see her often at market, her head-basket loaded with apples or cheeses or chickens or something."

"They are as poor as that!" cried the foreign lady.

"Poor? They are Basque farmers!" said the lawyer stiffly. "I am related to them myself."

He had been nettled all along by her attitude. What

114

had she expected? he asked himself irritably, running
his finger around under the tight-fitting edge of his
béret. A claim for rubies and railroad stocks out of the
Daranatz family at Yende-Onak? In a scornful formula familiar to him he thought, "How French of
her!"—correcting himself at once, for, of course, it was
obvious she was not French. Well, then, how un-
Basque! That was really what he meant, thought the
old Basque proudly, straining his ears to make out the
sense of what she was saying in that queer heavy
French of hers.

### III

In her low-heeled black Oxfords Miss Mary Haven
Palmer climbed slowly—she was not used to such
grades—up the steep, narrow road beyond Yende-
Onak. Through her pince-nez she surveyed with an
ironical expression the small, low, whitewashed farmhouse with wide-spreading roof which clung to the
rocks at the end of a still steeper side road, hardly
more than a stony path. A cow's head protruded from
one tiny window; geraniums in tomato cans stood on
the sill of the window next to it. As she turned off and
began to pick her way among the sharp-edged stones
of the path, a pig's forequarters appeared over the top

of a low wattled fence, small, deeply-set eyes staring at her out of a mud-smeared face. Miss Palmer stared back. "Gure Chocua," "Home of our forefathers," "Our hole," she murmured with a twist of her thin lips that did not add to their beauty.

Arrived, rather winded by the climb, in front of the house she hesitated. In the wide central opening hens scratched on a manure-pile. A lean black dog got up on his feet and looked at her in an ominous silence. "Whatever possessed me to let that old man tell them about me!" she thought impatiently. "Well, at least I made him understand that I'm not rich. They needn't think they'll get any money out of me."

A door at one side opened and two women came out, one young and one very old, both in black cotton dresses, each with a black kerchief twisted closely around her head. They came towards her, walking noiselessly in their flexible canvas sandals. She stood her ground ungraciously, looking at them hard from behind rimless eye-glasses. "What do they want out of me?" she asked herself, noticing now that the younger woman was what she had always called "an expectant mother." Were they perhaps "that kind" of folks? Miss Palmer heartily wished she were on her way back home to the High School where she belonged.

The older woman kissed her on both cheeks and said in French with as queer an accent as Miss Palmer's, "Welcome to Gure Chocua, *ma chère nièce.*" And the younger woman, saluting her ceremoniously in the same way, said, "You are welcome, Cousin." They led her back into the house, through a door over which, on the whitewashed stone framework, the date 1673 was crudely carved. Seeing her eyes on it, the older woman explained, "Yes, this is the new part of the house." Inside the low-ceilinged, whitewashed stone room there were set out on a heavy trestle-supported table a bottle and three glasses. They seated her beside the fireplace—if it was a fireplace. She had never seen anything like it, a platform of stone as high as a table, on which burned a tiny fire of twigs, accurately placed under a black kettle hanging from a crane. The three glasses were filled, the cork put back in the bottle. Her two hostesses lifted their glasses to hers. "Welcome home, *ma nièce,*" said the aged woman with dignity, drinking down her toast in one swallow.

Miss Palmer drank hers too, unsuspectingly, and felt as though she had swallowed Vesuvius in full eruption. Seeing her agonized look, watering eyes, and hand clutching at her paralyzed throat, the younger woman said, appreciatively, "Yes, isn't it good? Nobody can make Izarra as Gratien's grandmother can."

Miss Palmer in all her thirty-seven years had never drunk anything half so potent as this full dose of what Gratien's grandmother made. The room swam around her, the tall clock solemnly waltzing with the dark carved chest and the flag-bottomed chairs. She coughed hard, sneezed twice, blew her nose, and took hold firmly of the arm of her chair, having the impression that she was about to fall from it.

The older woman was making conversation politely. "Must you wear a hat?" she was asking pityingly. "I suppose, living in France, one must."

"Cousin Maï lives in America," the younger woman reminded her.

"Ah, yes. Buenos Aires?"

Miss Palmer, still incapable of speech, could only shake her head.

"You could take your hat off here," suggested the old woman, her eyes still on it as though its grotesqueness were more than she could endure. Like an automaton Miss Palmer took it off. Her hand caught in the black cord of her pince-nez and jerked them to the floor, where with an unheeded tinkle they broke into many pieces. The light from the window fell full on her face.

"Oh! Oh!" cried the old woman, her mannered ceremony disappearing. "Wait! Let me look!" Leaning forward, she gazed into the countenance of Miss Palmer, now unshaded by hat, shorn of eye-glasses. "Why! Why!" the old woman stammered, her lips shaking. "Terecha! Come here. Look! No, no, you're too young. You wouldn't remember." She rose to her feet, her eyes still on Miss Palmer's face. She passed her hands over her eyes as if to clear them. She cried out strange words, vehemently. She flung her arms out in a passionate gesture of welcome, and drawing Miss Palmer into them, she fell to weeping on her shoulder, saying brokenly, "You look like my Jeanne. Oh, *ma chère nièce*, you look just like my dead Jeanne come back to me."

## IV

It might have been—as indeed occurred to the surprised school-teacher the next morning, making her toilette in the clean, bare whitewashed bedroom under the eye of a brightly chromoed Our Lady of Lourdes—

the Izarra that got her into it. But it was not Izarra that made her stay, for since then she had had but an occasional swallow of sour cider with the soup and cheese of an evening. Mostly they drank milk. She stayed because she had found out the answer to the suspicious question she had put to herself as Tante Maï approached her. "What does she want out of me?" She knew now what Tante Maï wanted. It was something which in giving she took back tenfold, something she had never had from Palmer and Webster cousins—the feeling of kinship as a bond to be trusted beyond any trust Miss Palmer had ever known, save her childhood's certainty that her father and mother were incapable of wishing her anything but good. Tante Maï wished her well in that way. And took for granted that she could have no other feeling for the Daranatz of Gure Chocua.

It did not occur to the old woman that one Daranatz need explain or apologize to another for confiding troubles, for asking sympathy, for hoping for good counsel in difficulty. Her trouble was not even a personal matter, looked at from the Daranatz point of view, but a family affair that concerned any one of their blood. And till Petite Maï came back to them, there had been none of the family left to talk things over with, save Gratien and his little wife, both of them too young to understand life. "They are such children!" she often told her niece. "They do not think, as grown people would, that for always a Daranatz has lived here, for always we have been here, here, *here!*" She stamped her foot on the thin soil with the free expressive impulsiveness which made talking with her seem to her American great-niece almost like seeing an exciting play. It was evident that when she said "we" she meant "we," that it was herself who had lived there for a thousand years—a thousand? What were a thousand years? A mere French family could have lived for a thousand years on the same farm. "For *always we* have been here," she said, and meant it.

And now—she poured out the dark thoughts to her niece—if only Jeanne and her husband had lived, her daughter Jeanne, Gratien's mother, they would have all worked together, "could have held Gratien—or if even with his parents living he had been incurable, there would have been other children, another son, some one to—oh, if Jeanne had lived, never, never would there have been this talk of—" she could not finish the sentence. No, she could not bring out from her lips the words "selling the land," any more than she could have said, "selling my mother."

The first time this was said, Petite Maï asked, "Incurable? Gratien?" Gratien, supple and strong and hard, his clean white shirt open at the throat, his blue cotton trousers belted around his slim waist with a red sash, his agile feet in their white sandals, his round béret fitting close to his round dark head? What was the incurable disease of such a figure?

"Frivolity!" said his grandmother bitterly. And then, melting, "No, no, no, only youth." He should not have inherited the farm so young. If his parents had only lived to keep things going as parents should during the children's time of irresponsibility! Gratien was only what a young man, what a young Daranatz, should be. He worked on the farm, as much as a man in the flower of his age could! And beyond that what did he want? No harm. Only to be the best *pelota* player in the valley, to dance with his young wife at fiestas, to improvise verses of an evening with the other cider-drinkers in the village tavern, to run the mountains hunting for chamois, to play yet more *pelota*—she would not have a young Daranatz other than gay. But there should be parents to hold things together till he grew out of his gayety—and there was only this old, old grandmother, fit for nothing but to watch the cows! If during these heady years of youth he did as so many boys from their valley had done, grew exasperated with the poverty and hardship of his mountain farm, gave it all up, went down into the cities, worked in a factory, brought up the baby Daranatz, soon to come into the world, in rented rooms on wages, sold the—no, she still could not say it, not even through the hands pressed tightly over her face as she rocked to and fro on the grass in the high mountain pasture where she had guarded animals for thrice ten thousand years.

Miss Palmer, having lived all her life in Massachusetts factory towns or near them, and having an all too complete picture before her eyes of what bringing up babies in tenement houses on uncertain wages really meant, murmured a very genuine sympathy. "Yes, it would be terrible," she said, "for him to give up the dignity and freedom and health of this life for the miseries of an unskilled wage-earner's life." But that was not what had been in Tante Maï's mind. "It would be *terrible!*" she cried, clasping her hands together and raising them high before her, "terrible!—to abandon Gure Chocua."

It was, however, not always about her own troubles that Tante Maï talked. She was interested in Petite Maï and often tried to make her describe her strange life in America so that a home-keeping Basque could imagine it. Not with any success, as the questions often showed. She was sorry for her on many counts, Miss Palmer found.

Among others, for the queer clothes she had been forced to adopt. "How about wearing these *espadrilles?*" she said, offering her a pair of white canvas hemp-soled Basque shoes. Well, yes, Miss Palmer would try them. And having once tied them on her feet she never put her stiff, heeled leather Oxfords on again till the day at the end of summer when the inevitable leave-taking came, and, dressing again in her strange Millersburg costume, she took the diligence down to St. Jean Pied-de-Port, on the first stage of her journey back to her work in the High School. Her hair blew wildly in the mountain winds, and her hat would look too ridiculous, climbing up those steep, stony paths with Tante Maï, sitting beside her to watch the cows, weeding with her in the vegetable·garden or feeding the chickens. So her head was soon bound around with the decent black kerchief. And how about a dress of

Jeanne's, one of her black cottons that had been hanging in the closet since her death? "Surely it must be *hard* for a nice woman to appear in public in *those!*" said Tante Maï, looking shocked at the bright colors in the few simple dresses Miss Palmer had brought with her in the suitcase. The pince-nez had never been repaired since that first day. There are no opticians in Basque villages. Before Miss Palmer had been at Gure Chocua a week she was Petite Maï from head to foot. Standing with Tante Maï in the tiny *place* of Yende-Onak on a market day, she saw the old lawyer from St. Jean Pied-de-Port pass before them. It was evident that he had no idea who she was, for when she nodded, he gave her a vague salutation and the "Agur, anderia" with which he would have greeted a Basque.

Not having her eye-glasses, she could not read. And this was perhaps the strangest part of her strange summer. For the first time in her memory, day after day passed without her reading a word. It was almost like giving up a covering which had always been tightly wrapped around her. Day after day the layers of that covering were fewer. Things that had been hidden under them came into sight. Presently there came into sight some one she had always been, but had never met before.

Since there was no reading, evenings were mostly spent on the bench before the door. When they were there, the young people, Gratien and his wife Terecha, often sang, old Basque songs with minor cadences, "Ainhara," the swallow song, or "Zeruka izarenbidia," the way of the stars. But as Terecha's time drew nearer, they frequently went down together to the village to sit quietly with her mother. The two Maï's, left alone, looked up at the stars over the black mountain across the valley from them, or down at the lighted windows of the village houses far below them. In these long, still hours together they talked, in their queer French, of all kinds of things, mostly of things Miss Palmer had never heard mentioned in talk—of life and death and sin and love—things that two women, one old and one no longer young, should think of. The unknown self that had been hidden so long under printed words spoke out from Miss Palmer's lips in musings and ponderings and searchings after understanding. One evening, sitting so in the dusk, a faint breeze blowing up to them from the hay fields of the valley, Petite Maï found herself telling Tante Maï what she had never even told herself before, that she had not married because no man had ever loved her. The tears fell down over her cheeks as she said it, tears that had lain on her heart for years.

"Did you ever love any man?" Tante Maï asked her.

But no! how could she have loved if no one had loved her first! It was Miss Palmer who said this quickly. But even as she heard the words, she was Petite Maï who knew what the old woman meant. Her heart widened then, burst from the Palmer and Webster barriers that had held it cramped so long, and she wept silently and blessedly in the darkness, no longer out of wounded vanity but in a sorrow so noble that it was almost as comforting as a joy, the sorrow that she had missed love, not only that love had missed her.

v

As she followed Tante Maï about, helping her in the queer perpendicular farming that took place at Gure Chocua, Petite Maï saw many many things she did not understand. Why, for instance, must their two patient cows, beasts of burden as well as milk-givers, never be yoked for work without being draped in a certain coarsely woven white linen cloth with certain blue and

127

red stripes running down the middle? When they were led out to go to pasture, nobody dreamed of putting on these ceremonial cloths. But they were as necessary as their yoke, apparently, to their doing any work. Why was this? She asked this, her first question, casually, in all confidence, expecting a reasonable explanation which had not occurred to her citified ignorance of farm ways. But she encountered on the faces of her Basque kin the expression which means, "You evidently just don't understand the nature of things or you wouldn't ask!" They looked with a puzzled expression from her to the linen-draped cattle. She repeated her words. Then they told her, with an intonation of almost breathless astonishment over her question, "Why, it's *always* put on Basque oxen and cows!" And no more was to be had out of them, then or later, on this or any other matter, save some variations on this formula. Neither did she ever learn why, no matter how hot the day, a heavy blue-dyed sheepskin must always lie on top of the yoke. Nor why a long bright-colored fringe must hang down over the cow's eyes. "To keep the flies away!" she surmised, but gave up this attempt at reasoning from cause to effect when she learned the fringe was worn winter as well as summer. Nor why on

the twenty-third of every June, at least one person
from each house in the region must make the tiresome
trip to Cambo to drink as much water as possible while
the clock strikes midnight—at the same time filling
bottles with the same water to bring home to those
unable to go. Nor why on the second Sunday in September, every one who could manage it made the even
longer trip to Biarritz, to bathe in the ocean on a certain rough, unsheltered beach deserted for the rest of
the year. Nor why every Basque *makhila* must be just
the same. The *makhila* is the combination of ox-goad
and walking-stick and sword, without which no Basque
ever leaves his own land. Apparently to prevent the
wood from splintering, every *makhila* is bound in brass,
and on every one the brass is graven in exactly the same
odd design of interwoven lines. But although this
binding was of brass, every *makhila* was tipped at the
end with copper. Why the *two* metals? Turning
Gratien's *makhila* around in her hand one day, she
asked him this, idly. He explained stiffly, with almost
a pained look, "Why, *nobody* would want to carry a
*makhila* without a copper tip!"

After a good many experiences of this kind she perceived that although they tried to hide it, these ques-

tions were slightly shocking to them; as when a child, though ever so innocently, blurts out casual words about a subject too sacred to be anything but hidden. So after a time she stopped asking questions, even when she saw something which puzzled her very much indeed, as did a little ceremony which was an invariable part of the occasional expedition up to the highest of their three bits of pasture land. This lay on a grassy shelf, high above the tiny plateau on which Gure Chocua lay. The ladder-like path turned to the right after a time, climbed still higher, led around the shoulder of the mountain, skirting the base of a precipitous mass of rocks that was almost a cliff, and came out beyond, upon the two-acre pasture. Tante Maï evidently had a special liking for the trip up to this place. When the day came around on which the cows were to be taken there, her brown, withered-apple old face always shone peacefully.

It was so far from the house that they never planned to come home for lunch but took along a big chunk of *arto*, the bread made from maize eaten by Basques alone among Europeans, a slab of cheese, and a bottle of milk. As they came to the foot of the cliff, Tante Maï always stopped the little procession of two cows and two women. Reaching into the bag where the lunch was packed, she broke off a piece of the cheese and took out the bottle of milk. Climbing up then, a few steps, on some broken points, she laid the cheese carefully on a certain bowlder with a flat top, and slowly sprinkled a little milk around it in a circle.

She did this with a manner so grave and decent, with a face so composed and thoughtful, so—one might almost say—devout, that it imposed silence on her American niece, waiting for her on the path below. What would be the use of asking why that was done? She knew the Basque answer already. "Why, we have always done it." She did not ask this question, but she thought about it a great deal in the long, sunny, beatifically empty hours on the upland pasture, as she lay in the grass beside Tante Maï, sitting upright, drawing out and twisting a thread from the ball of fluffy white wool thrust through the head of her distaff. One day the American, taking this ancient woman's tool into her hands, noticed the ornamentation on it, a design of interwoven lines, lightly burned into the wood. She said casually, without reflection, "This design is just the same as that on the brass of Gratien's *makhila*, isn't it?"

Before the old woman answered her, she was aware of that aura—what was it? Disapproval? Shocked reverence? "They look," she thought, "the way I'd feel to see children racing around, playing tag over the graves in a cemetery."

When Tante Maï spoke she said neutrally, "It's the same." Her intonation added an "Of course it is!" Her American niece handed back the distaff and lay down on the grass again, thinking of graves. There must be so many in this valley that the very grass under you, as you lay down in it anywhere, grew out of a vanished ancestor. "My ancestors, too," thought the American dreamily, watching the slow circles of an eagle. "I too have herded animals here for tens of thousands of years. I have lain here happily on this grass, felt myself part of this mountain—" For the first time she really shared Tante Maï's fear, was transfixed as by a knife by the fear that perhaps young Gratien would weary of the pinching life of a poor mountain farmer, would succumb to high wages and town life, would— no, she could not, any more than Gratien's grandmother, even say "sell the land." How horrible, how unbearable if—she lay there, silently consigning factories and high wages to eternal perdition with a heat that would have astonished the people in her High School if they had known of it.

Beside her Tante Maï continued to spin. She held the distaff thrust through her belt and steadied by her left hand, while with her right she continually drew out the thread, keeping the spindle spinning rapidly with a twist of her fingers. Her American niece had often noticed that the intent gaze on the twirling spindle put Basque spinners almost into an hypnotic trance. Looking up now at the old woman, she saw that her lips moved slightly once in a while as if she were saying something to herself. Finding her niece's dreamy eyes on her, she smiled a little and said in a low murmuring voice, "It's nice here, isn't it, in the old Gure Chocua?"

In her niece's mind there rang so loudly a sharp "What's that? What are you saying?" that she shrank together, fearing Tante Maï's startled gaze on her. But there was no echo in the thin, bright mountain air. She had not spoken, she had only thought that breath-less exclamation. She crossed her forearms over her face as if to shut out the sun, and behind this screen began to think. Not deep, wordless Daranatz thoughts now, but energetic Webster and Palmer ones that

stepped firmly and logically from one idea to the one
that followed on it, no matter where it took her. Presently she took down her arms from over her face.
Stiffly. She had lain there in the same position a long
time. She sat up and asked in a low, hushed, unem-
phasized tone, as though she were speaking to a sleep-
walker, "*Is* this the old Gure Chocua?"

But the tone was not quiet enough. Tante Maï
started a little, looked at her, looked away, and said,
after a moment's pause, "My grandmother called it
that sometimes."

### VI

The Basque woman with a weather-beaten tanned
face, clad in a plain black dress and close-folded black
headkerchief, stepping down the steep mountain road
in her hemp-soled *espadrilles* with a long, free, flexible
gait, did not look like Miss Palmer of Millersburg, but
it was really she again. She was on her way to Yende-
Onak as fast as she could get there, to catch the diligence down to St. Jean Pied-de-Port to the old lawyer's
office. And as she swung along she was rehearsing in her
mind—to be sure to get her tenses and subjunctives
right—what she was going to tell the old lawyer. "A
chance remark of Tante Maï's put me on the track,

and without saying anything to her or Gratien—you
know how queer Basques are about some things—I
went back the next day by myself to the place on that
cliff path where Tante Maï always left the ceremonial
food. The moment I really looked, with this idea in my
mind, at the pieces of rock where she steps up, it was
perfectly plain they were what was left of an old path
up the face of the cliff. So I started up. It was hard
going at first, but before long it was plainly a path
that wound around a sort of buttress projecting from
the cliff. And when I turned the corner around that,
I saw—"

Here Miss Palmer's heart gave a quite unexpected
plunge in her breast like the one she had felt when she
had turned that corner and saw— She began to walk
more slowly, living over what she had seen as well as
planning how she would tell it. Those sentences she
was planning began to be blurred, to break off in the
middle: "I had brought candles, of course, thinking
that if I really did— I lighted one. The wind outside
blew it out instantly. So I waited and lighted it again
as soon as I had stepped inside. The air was as still—
as still—"

The brown-faced woman in the black headkerchief

stood still herself on the hot, dusty summer road. The
wind blew hard up the valley, as it always did, flutter-
ing her skirts. She gazed fixedly before her, seeing the
steady spear-shaped flame of a candle burning in a
breathless quiet. Holding it in her hand, she walked
slowly forward between the rock walls, darkening as
she left the opening behind her, down the long pas-
sage that sloped beneath her feet and turned around
on itself. And now it was all black around the candle's
steady flame. She lifted it high to see where the pas-
sage led. And once more she began to tremble from
head to foot as she saw them there, the great forms
painted on the walls, the deer with delicate uplifted
forefoot, raising its victim's dove's eyes to her, the
fierce male vitality of the red-brown buffalo caught in
mid-charge, the strange, unknown, shaggy-maned animals with foretops hanging low over their eyes like a
fringe—in her shaking hand the candle flame wavered,
and in its changing light they came to life, breathed,
shifted their places, looked at her. Shudder after shudder of excitement ran over the woman gazing back at
them. What power, what a splendor of life in every
swelling muscle and hard, supporting bone! And when
she recognized the design of interwoven lines like a

frieze above them, the skin all over her body contracted sharply in a spasm which ran like ice-water at
the roots of her hair.

Some one was shouting at her!

She gave a great start, but was so far out of her
body that she could not find it again, could not stir.
She turned her head from side to side blindly, groping
through millenniums of time to find the body which
was hers for this her present life.

Some one seized her firmly and drew her with a
friendly roughness to one side. It was the driver of an
ox-team which had all but pushed the pole of their
cart into her as she stood there rooted to the hot dusty
road. He laughed good-naturedly at her dazed face as
she slowly came back to herself, said something in
Basque with a smile, and walked on, light-footed, supple, swinging his *makhila*, its graven brass binding
flashing in the sun. The oxen swung slowly by, the
ceremonial fringe dangling over their eyes.

The woman they had left behind drew one long un-
even breath after another, tremblingly smoothing down
her black headdress in a meaningless, mechanical gesture. Finally turning about, she trudged slowly back
up the road to Gure Chocua. She was in no state to talk

business to a lawyer, thought Miss Palmer, excusing her retreat to herself.

But things at Gure Chocua were in no state to tranquilize shaken nerves. Little Terecha's time was nearly there; she was frightened and tearful, and young Gratien was worse. The season was especially crowded just then with farm work, the maize fields needing their last hoeing, the second crop of hay ready to be cut and brought in by hand from the inaccessible pockets of soil among the rocks where it grew. Everything Gratien did went wrong, and although he did not burst into tears as Terecha did when a dish slipped from her fingers, he burst into curses against farm work, against Gure Chocua. He would sell the accursed stoneheap the moment the baby was born, and move to Bordeaux or Bilbao and work in the factories. He would bring the child up never to hear the name of the place that had bled them all white. And he hoped it would be a girl who could not even think of going on as he had. Tante Maï watched him miserably as he muttered away, and he watched the pale, suffering Terecha.

Petite Maï watched them all three, and sometimes, pitching hay down to the cows and feeding the hens, surprised herself by groaning aloud. She made one determined effort to influence Gratien, choosing the time when he was mending the door to the hen-house and Terecha was near enough to hear.

"See here, Gratien, I know more about factory towns and factory life than you do. You think you have it hard here. But you'd have it harder there! You'd cut your throat in six months' time. An independent land-owning man like you, who's never had rent to pay, who's never depended on a job. To live in two or three cramped little rooms—and those likely to be taken away from you the instant you didn't have cash to pay for them, to buy every morsel of food you and the family eat, to see your children running with vicious playfellows because there is nowhere for them to play but the street. To have to bow your Basque head to take the orders, and endure the injustice perhaps, of a man you despise, because he has more money and is your employer. And to have no escape, no roof of your own, to feel that your family's very life depends on your taking meekly—you, a Basque!—what some French or Spanish boss pleases to give you in the way of curses and—"

But he was not even listening to her—swearing

viciously under his breath as he wrenched off the hinge
he had put on crookedly.

So Miss Palmer tried it again, setting off down the
road with something of the old Millersburg expression
of reliability on her firmly set lips. She would not this
time allow her nerves to get the better of her, she would
not in imagination retrace her steps into that opening
in the cliff face, the very thought of which sent her
pulse up to unsteady speed. It was a simple matter of
business to discuss with a lawyer.

"I have discovered on my cousin's land a cave with
cave-paintings on the walls. Like those in the Dor-
dogne, only finer; like those in the Spanish cave, from
illustrations I've seen. Very stirring. Astonishingly sure
drawing and powerful coloring. Now whether my
cousin and aunt know about this I can't tell—you
know how queer Basques are about some things—perhaps they don't know whether they know, *surely*.
Everybody in the village must know—if you can call
it knowing—where their set of old customs come from,
the designs on the *makhilas* and the distaffs, the fringe
for their oxen like the foretops of those—" No, no, she
must not go into detail like this. The lawyer was a

Basque too and would be deeply offended—if you could say it was offense they felt. She went back to the plain, bare certainty of business is business. "But what I do know is that they do not realize that this is a very very valuable piece of property. And they are very poor people who terribly need money. All I need from you is good legal advice about how to organize the matter so that their interests will be secured against exploitation. There will be, of course, as soon as it is known, a rush of savants and later of tourists. I have visited such caves elsewhere in France and know something about how it is managed." Here a picture of how it was managed came vividly before her eyes: the crowds of gaping tourists, the vapid remarks, the attempts to carve names on the rock walls, the jokers with their slimy remarks about those boldly realistic animals, male and female, the spoiled children rubbing their hands on the paintings, the skeptics who audibly knew it was a fake. She shook her head and went on resolutely with her planning. "There will be need to be, of course, a person at the entrance to take in the admission fee, and to go with the visitors to show them the frescoes, and probably receive a tip afterward. Now I want, even if the Government should declare the cave the property of the state, to make sure that my cousin's wife and my aunt will have those positions." The thought of Tante Maï offered a tip for showing the old Gure Chocua to foreign strangers brought out from her a horrified groan.

But strong-willed Palmers and Websters, used to mastering material situations, with their centuries of faith in common sense, were not yet beaten. They carried her steadily forward till she stood in the dusty, stony little *place* of Yende-Onak at the spot where the diligence to St. Jean Pied-de-Port passed. "There will be the question of the rights of reproduction, of course," she went on, rehearsing her speech to the old lawyer, "postcards and souvenirs, you know. I want to be sure that the sale of those—" At the thought of those mighty, secret, sacred masterpieces dwarfed to postcard size, scrawled on by idle excursionists, all the Daranatz in her broke out in a shamed cold sweat.

"See here," Miss Palmer sternly told Petite Maï, "it's not a question of feelings or what one would like to do. It's a simple question of keeping a Daranatz at Gure Chocua. There's no other way. No matter how, is better than not at all, isn't it? If Tante Maï can't, I will."

She held her kerchiefed head high at this.

But when the diligence came along she was not there to get into it. For, astoundingly, into the *place* there had swung the yoked, fringed, blue-sheepskinned heads of the two cows from Gure Chocua, her two cows; she knew them perfectly. In the cart behind sat Tante Maï, ·bending over some one, and beside the cattle, striking the point of his *makhila* viciously into the ground with every step, and looking very nervous and white, strode Gratien. Terecha's time had come. She was being taken to her mother's.

The diligence came and departed; the sun rose higher and sank lower, sank finally behind the mountain on which Gure Chocua lay deserted. The stars came out, blazing mountain stars wheeling slowly through a black sky over the heads of the young father and his cousin, sitting out before the house in the village. Tante Maï was inside, too useful to be spared. With the Daranatz family diminished as it was, there would have been nobody at all to sit with young Gratien through that night if Petite Maï had not come from America to join them.

He smoked a great many cigarettes at first, rolling

them rapidly out of his smuggled Spanish tobacco, taking a whiff or two and suddenly throwing them away as though they made him sick. And at first he was perpetually springing up to go inside the tiny house on tiptoe to listen at the door of the inner room to the voices and groans which came through it. Muttering wild Basque oaths, he came back to roll another cigarette and throw it away. Or he paced up and down before the house, his hands over his ears. But as the night wore on and the constellations slowly rose and sank, he ended by falling exhausted on the bench beside his cousin, finally even laying his head on her shoulder and weeping silently, nervous, helpless exasperated angry tears. She wiped them gently away as they fell, drawing him closer to her, her head sometimes bent over his, sometimes raised to the old quiet of the stars, looking down on yet another Daranatz birth.

They must have fallen asleep finally, for it seemed to be from another world that Petite Maï heard the door behind them open. Dawn had come. The stars had gone. The mountains stood up all around the village. Tante Maï appeared, bowed almost double with exhaustion. Over the young man's head Petite Maï looked her question. Tante Maï was too tired to smile, but she nodded and formed three words with her lips. Petite Maï leaned to Gratien's ear.

"Wake up, young father," she murmured. "Wake up. Terecha is safe. And you have a son."

He came to his feet with one bound, looking from her to his grandmother.

"A son!" he said, and looked around him at the mountains. "A son!"

He passed both hands up and down over his face as if to rub off the memory of the night.

"A *son!*" he cried to the two women, announcing it as though he were the bringer of the news.

He turned to his grandmother and said, "Now we have an heir to Gure Chocua."

Tante Maï stood up then, straight as any girl, and brought her hands together high before her, shaking them in a noiseless ecstasy.

He turned to his cousin. "We will name him after your grandfather, because he died in exile," he said. "We will name him Juanech Daranatz."

He came closer to her, looking at her with shining eyes, and with a grand, proud gesture said, "I invite you, cousin, to be godmother to the future owner of Gure Chocua, our home."

People back in Millersburg asked each other if the teacher of French in the High School didn't look different this year somehow, or did they just imagine it? Perhaps it was because she had got herself very sunburned. "What a beautiful tan you did get!" they often said to her.

She explained, "I spent the summer with some relatives who live on a farm in the country."

"Well, it surely did do you lots of good."

"Yes," she agreed, soberly, "I think it did. I expect to be with them, summers, quite often, now."

Once some one added, looking at her hard and trying to decide what there *was* about her in these days— "It's very becoming, that tan. Makes you look ten years younger."

To which Miss Palmer answered with an odd, secret, proud smile that made her look younger yet, "Does it? I don't feel so. I feel older. Very much older indeed."

sand. As dreamily as I, the customs guard too observed the landing. He roused himself from where he had sat smoking and sunning himself on the sea-wall, stretched, sauntered down to the water's edge, blinked, scratched himself, then with a glance at the pile of glistening fish, nodded a "pretty good luck, boys," and strolled off, lighting a fresh cigarette.

Memories of the bitter, virtuous U.S.A. energy of our own customs inspectors broke the spell of my vacuity and contentment.

"How can he have the face to draw pay for inspections like that?" I asked the world. "It's not an hour's row to the Spanish coast. For all he knows, under those fish the boat is full of Spanish lace and tobacco."

"Perhaps it is," murmured my companion comfortably. "But it's quite inspection enough to give Basques fishing in their own waters."

There it was again! Because their kinfolk live and always have lived on both sides of it, they ignore—and for the most part successfully—the existence of the boundary line between France and Spain. They and their airs of superiority to ideas swallowed whole by the rest of the docile twentieth century!

One of the fishermen, a neighbor whose children

often played with mine, now came striding past us on his way to the path up the cliff. He gave me a nod and saluted my friend with the amusing respect which some grown men keep for their boyhood teachers. I smiled at the contrast between his schoolboy look at her and his magnificent proportions. He owned the finest pair of shoulders in the settlement, tapering to a slim waist, supple under its broad leather belt. The school-teacher looked after him meditatively as he sped up the long, winding, rocky path at the true Basque gait, supple and poised and rhythmic as if he were a Russian ballet dancer dancing a fancy step.

"How long has this fashion for wearing *espadrilles* existed among the Basques?" I asked idly.

"What a question!" answered the school-teacher with a sleepy laugh. "Since Neolithic days, of course. And what a word—'fashion'! What does it mean? Nothing to a Basque. That's perhaps why nervous prostration is unknown among us: no fashions to keep up to."

"Ah," I thought to myself, impatiently, "now we'll hear some more about Basque superiority! But I shall rebel, and at the top of my voice, if she tells me again that story about the devil's coming here to lead the

Basques astray as he had the rest of the world, and having to give up because he couldn't learn their language."

But no, it was not that old story which she now brought out as she roused herself to talk and sat up straighter. She was still on the subject of *espadrilles*.

"Is it possible," she asked me, "that you have lived amongst us for months and have not yet had quoted to you the earliest Roman mention of Basques, in which their agility and sure-footedness is spoken of as almost superhuman? Doesn't that show we were wearing *espadrilles* and playing *pelote* then as now? And that then as now a Basque boy could run down a mountain path at a speed that breaks a goat's leg? It is not by chance that Basques are sure-footed. Nothing is by chance. It is a part of our philosophy, our non-Aryan philosophy, not to fight against things as they are, or to try to escape from them into some imagined unreality, but to do what we can with them. Take feet, for instance. A very important subject in human life, though so neglected elsewhere. We have not dreamed, during century after century, of trying to invent ever-changing foot-gear which will make feet look as though they were not feet. Nor of giving by ornamentation a

false surface beauty to those strange inventions. No;
being born with feet, we do not rebel against them.
We use them. We love them. We make the best of
them. And believe me, the best is very good." She
stretched out her beautiful, slim, shapely feet in their
*espadrilles*, flexing and turning them till they looked
like little white birds ready to fly. "To walk about the
world well poised on supple feet in perfect shoes—it is
a Basque joy of every hour, of every age in every
human life. It is, you will say, one of the smaller joys.
But those small joys are precious consolations for
existing, and this one is an active pleasure, simple,
honest, harmless, and ever renewed. It has always been
as open to all of humanity as to Basques. We are not
the only race with feet. But no other civilized literate
people, not one, I think, has kept the primitive pleasure
in good feet. Quite the contrary. Quite tragically the
contrary. With no reason in the world for it, the others
have made a penalty of walking, a long, painful pun-
ishment. The descriptions of the pain and torture
caused by leather shoes with heels—you see it in all
Aryan publications in the advertisements of manufac-
turers who make money out of corn cures and foot-
care—it turns me as sick with sympathy and horror as

the descriptions of the racks and wheels of the Inquisi-
tion. At least those tortures were inflicted in a mis-
guided effort to save human souls. These modern foot-
tortures—but I don't need those written descriptions.
After a day in an Aryan city—Paris, Lyons—I sink
into my bed exhausted for what I have seen all day:
those wretched brothers and sisters of mine, stumping
dismally about on atrophied feet, tilted forward on
wooden pegs, bound by unyielding leather into the
likeness of something carved in wood. Note that as
soon as a well-to-do European sees that his feet are
asserting themselves against their leather prisons, sees
that they are ever so little shaping his foot-gear into the
shape of a human foot—he goes hurriedly and buys a
new pair. Where else in the civilized world would you
find such a collection of strong, living, contented,
happy feet as those which carry us Basques blithely
about, as comfortably in our old age as in childhood?
To take what life gives you and make the best of it
according to its own nature—why isn't that as good
as struggling to make it different from what it is, and
then in addition always trying to make it different
today from what you made it yesterday? For that is
what you call 'fashion,' isn't it?"

"You're talking Basque," I told her.

"No doubt," she replied; "it is, after all, the only language I really know." She tried to say this with humility. But she did not at all succeed.

Well, I like *espadrilles* myself—never wear anything else if I can help it. I could not very well select this particular burst of Basque eloquence as the occasion for my protest. But as she talked, it had risen perceptibly nearer the surface of my mind.

Chance offered me my occasion, and at that very moment. As we looked we saw the climbing fisherman disappear over the top of the cliff where the roof of a cottage showed its red tiles against the sky. At once a horrid discord of wrangling voices shattered the golden quiet. To be exact, one horrid discordant shrill voice and a bass murmur.

"I can't imagine why Jean-Pierre lets that lazy, bad-tempered wife tyrannize over him so," I said wonderingly. "She's a terror if there ever was one. I heard his cousin say in the store this morning that she's left him nothing of his own but his skin, and some day she'll take that for her dish-rag." I turned to my companion. "All Basques too," I reminded her. "Not a drop of Aryan blood anywhere. You'll have to admit that even among Basques—"

She was no longer looking either pleasantly vacuous, beatific, or complacent. Rather grim. She did not pick up my challenge with her usual spirit.

"Alas!" she murmured, hiding her proud feet humbly under her skirts. "What are we, any of us, but human beings? You do well to remind me of that unescapable fact. But in truth, I should need no reminder from you. A date approaches which is sufficient—" She looked over at me ironically. "You might enjoy that story. It proves Basques to be not superior at all, but helplessly like all other humans. Yes, exactly." She added dryly, "It even has in it, to suit your taste, one very bad Basque as well as a lot of foolish ones. In fact, for good measure, now I think of it, two very bad Basques. Not a pennyworth to choose between them, in my opinion, although one of them was an example of those ornaments of church and state known as completely devoted mothers.

"I never saw her. She died long ago, a couple of years before I ever came to Itsasmendia. But I didn't need to see her to know her. You'll know her too, without any description, as soon as I tell you the mere facts of her life. You've seen her like often enough elsewhere. She married somebody or other who soon died, leaving her with one little boy, to whom she 'gave her whole life.' You know what that formula means, that she wanted his whole life in return. When he was old enough—nineteen or twenty; Basques marry young— he fell in love in his turn with somebody or other, a nice girl of the neighborhood just like anybody. Except in his mother's eyes. That devoted saint had at once some passionate tragic objection to her, such as mothers who have given their whole lives to only sons have against the girls their sons love. I've forgotten what. Didn't like the color of her eyes, perhaps, or maybe the girl held her knitting needles wrong or put her mantilla on too far back, or some other low vice such as completely devoted mothers always detect. Remember that this took place a generation, two generations, ago. I only saw the very end of it and never heard the details of the beginning beyond the fact that nobody else could see anything the matter with the girl. That didn't prevent the young man's mother from falling into hysterics—literal hysterics—at any mention of her name, and absolutely forbidding the marriage.

"You know, until very lately the French law has

not allowed anybody under thirty to marry against his parents' wishes. So with the help of the law the mother kept those hungry young hearts starved and thwarted for ten interminable years. Even French law admitted that they were then old enough to run their own lives. But by that time the mother had worked up a case of nervous invalidism, with a bad heart that threatened to give way at any emotion. You've seen cases, very likely, of that kind of heart. The young lover—not so young now—was a dutiful son, a good Catholic, anxious to do his duty. This sweetheart was a dutiful girl, a good Catholic, anxious not to be selfish. The years dragged on, something always about to be done, some desperate resolution about getting married at once always taken—always checkmated by his mother's timely dramatic sinking spells. Who could risk marrying over his mother's corpse?

"Finally she did die. Perhaps her heart really had been bad. Yes, certainly, from all points of view it must have been very bad. Her son was then thirty-seven, his fiancée thirty-eight. They waited a year to pay due deference to the memory of that exemplary matron and then were married. At the end of the first year the wife, forty then, died in childbirth. Did the doctor really tell her husband, as the neighbors reported, that she would have been all right fifteen years younger? Or was that only the to-be-expected village talk? I don't know. It certainly was village gossip, for I arrived in town just at that time and heard nothing else.

"That funeral was the first thing I saw of Itsasmendia. I was very young, very sensitive to life. Perhaps now it would not sear my heart so horridly—the aspect of the husband, I mean. For weeks afterward I was pursued in my dreams by his fierce eyes fixed on nothingness, his strange swagger as he lurched his way forward at the head of the funeral procession. The others were sad-faced men with bent heads and sobbing women continually wiping away their tears from under their long black veils. But the bereaved husband held his head angrily high, and as he walked into the church swung his shoulders defiantly like a man going out to fight his most hated enemy. All through the long funeral service I could not take my eyes from that horrifying head of his, the jaw clenched, the eyes burning. It was the face of a man drunk with rebelliousness. I remember praying with all my heart for him, praying that he might resign himself and submit to the will of God. Yes, that is what I called it. The will of God. I was very young.

"As long as the sickly baby lived he lived, sitting silently by the cradle. The night the child died he walked off that cliff yonder. For years I never passed here without seeing how he must have done it, lurching along the path with that preoccupied air of inner fury. Not even troubling to fling himself off, just taking one too many of those heavy, forward-thrusting steps."

She looked up at the cliff and put a hand over her eyes. When she took it away she told me, with a little movement of her head as though to shake off an old shadow:

"In short, the episode made, as you can see, quite an impression on my young mind, was one of those lessons by which as we live we learn what sort of world we inhabit.

"Well, during a good many years I went on as one does in even the quietest life, accumulating information about that world. That information little by little turned me into the woman you know, who is a different person from the heart-shaken girl praying in the church at that funeral for the submission of the frantic man to the will of God. I had, after a time, rather different

—certainly less positive—ideas as to what the will of God might be.

"Perhaps my steadiest source of information about people was living intimately with many children. There is no training like a school-teacher's life for acquiring an X-ray eye. (If that's the kind of eye you want! It has its disadvantages!) The look of a child with a secret misdeed on his mind and the turbid look of a man with something to conceal—they are comically alike. I am always surprised that other people can't spot it as I do. But of course they haven't had my advantages for observation. When, twelve or thirteen years ago, I was invited by the Beheretche family to take supper at the farm and meet the father of Katicha, their granddaughter and one of my pupils, I was really taken aback by the infatuated credulity with which they accepted their son-in-law at his own estimate.

"It is true he was almost a stranger to them, having come into Itsasmendia from a distant commune only a short time before his marriage, and almost at once after the death of Katicha's mother going to Marseilles to live. For that matter, I knew nothing about him either—but one look at him was enough. The confiding

old people at the Beheretche farm were dazzled by
their elegant, affable guest in a coat and vest, with a
hat of stiff straw and shoes of stiff leather, quite like a
French tourist. He and I took to each other as warmly
as—well, did you ever see the meeting of a strange
cat and dog? I don't mean that I actually scratched his
face or that he literally showed his fangs. But our encounter was along the lines of 'How do you do, monsieur?' 'Enchanted to meet you, mademoiselle.' And
under the surface—not very far under—'What is that
man up to? What does he really want?' and 'Damn
that meddling woman! What did they have to bring
her into it for!'

"Anybody less guileless than the old farm people
would have found something fishy in his sudden effu-
sive reappearance just when his daughter was old
enough to become a wage-earner instead of a burden.
But I did not need such obvious grounds for suspicion.
No, the eye in the man's head was enough for an old
teacher. As I sorted over past memories of the schoolroom his expression was not, it seemed to me, the furtive, unhappy, rather touching look of a normally good
boy with a toad in his pocket or a broken window on
his conscience. It was rather the brazenly candid ex-

pression of the confirmed bad egg, the vicious boy with a string of nasty words in his memory, evil purposes in his heart, and enough oily lies on his tongue to make him more than a match for anything you can say to him. That was the impression he made on me. As for the impression I made on him, it was plain that he considered my existence, especially my presence as a friend of his family-in-law, one of the worst errors ever committed by Providence.

"Thin as was the veneer of our formal politeness, the Beheretche grandparents did not see through it. The decencies were kept up. I remained silent, and he talked smoothly of his purpose in coming. He had, he told us, the intention of doing many fine things for Katicha. She was then between fourteen and fifteen, just the age to take on polish and accomplishments. Excellent! She was to live with him in his prosperous Marseilles home. She would have silk stockings and patent leather slippers, eat meat twice a day, have wheat bread instead of maize, have her hair dressed by a coiffeur, ride on street cars, wear a hat to mass instead of a mantilla, and indulge in many other bourgeois gentilities. The Beheretches already saw their red-cheeked, chubby little Katicha a great lady.

162

"What had I against the benevolent plan? Nothing
except the way the man's eye, meeting mine squarely
enough, veiled itself and became opaque. I scarcely
ventured to mention so groundless an uneasiness to the
delighted old farmers, but finding myself alone with
them while the father strolled out to smoke an after-
dinner cigar, I did hesitatingly put it to them—wasn't
it just a little queer he should have paid no attention
to his child all the time she was a helpless dependent,
and now when she was big and strong and able to earn
money, should come to claim her? 'You know,' I said,
'anything she earns is legally his until she comes of age.
How can you be sure that his intention is not to set her
at work in some factory or shop and pocket her wages?
Or to use her as an unpaid drudge in his own household?'

"They were quite shocked by my suspiciousness.
Her own father! Who so plainly wanted to do his
duty by her! Why wouldn't he treat her well? Who
would be more likely to than her own father?

"Well, all right, I thought. It's no concern of mine.
It was true that Katicha had been in my schoolroom
for eight or nine years so that I felt that I had partly
brought her up. But that was equally true of almost

every other little girl in town. I couldn't go making myself responsible for them all, especially those who had perfectly solvent grandparents with farms and prosperous fathers to look out for them. Katicha herself was dancing with excitement and impatience to be off into her wonderful new life. Who was I? A grumpy old-maid school-teacher.

"I repeated these reasonable remarks to myself every time I saw Katicha or her father the next day or two, and turned my mental back resolutely on them. But there is rather more to one's inner workings than mental backs and fronts.

"The day of Katicha's departure I was with all the other Itsasmendia folks down at the railway station to see her off. But unlike the rest of them I had a small valise with me and a third-class ticket to Marseilles replacing twenty-six perfectly good francs in my pocketbook. I mentioned to the Beheretche old people (who were delighted to hear it) and to Katicha's father (who made no comment on the news) that I had for a long time been meaning to make a visit to a cousin of mine living in Marseilles, and thought I'd take this chance to have company on the trip. God forgive the lie—thought I—you can't fight the devil with holy water! I added to Granny Beheretcha in a good loud audible tone, 'When I get back I'll tell you all about Katicha's new home.' "

The school-teacher paused to laugh.

"If I had any gift for narrative I could make my fortune out on an account of the humors of the all-day and all-night trip in one and another third-class carriage to Marseilles. Those two bristling grown-ups, silently hating each other and exchanging black looks over Katicha's unconscious head! But I have no imagination. I never can think of anything to tell about an event more than the mere facts. In this case, no need to tell you even all of the facts, all the ups and downs of that fantastic journey—the changes, the waitings, the runnings up and down on station platforms, and finally the arrival at Marseilles. The only thing that matters is that during every minute of our endless traveling I could feel that man's mind alternating between the struggle to think of a plausible reason for getting rid of me and some other idea about me which I couldn't guess. I found out what it was a little later. A sufficiently unexpected notion too!

"Of course Katicha's natural clinging to me was the strength of my position. Why wouldn't she? Still a little shy of her new father, she chattered to me rather than to him, shared with me the hard-boiled eggs and corn bread I'd taken along, went to sleep with her head on my lap, and exclaimed many times over the good luck which had brought her old school-teacher along with them.

"Along with them the old teacher grimly stuck, too, through several attempts on that man's part to throw me off, through a feint at the terminal station in Marseilles of leaving me at a hotel and a pretense of taking Katicha to one—stuck along with them to the moment when, having by my bland persistence worn him out to a glaring exasperation, I stepped into the cab with them.

"When I stepped out, at the address he had given the driver, I found myself looking up at the façade of a shabby gray stucco house. There were others like it on the dingy street, but at the first sight of that particular house . . . was it because the windows were all closely shuttered? Or because of the iron bars over those on the ground floor? Or because the front door was very heavy and . . . No, that's trying to sound reasonable and probable. The plain fact is that I received an actual physical impression from that house,

as unmistakable to my senses as though I had heard or
smelled it. It may not have come from the house. Perhaps it was the bursting into flame of what had been
slowly smoldering in my mind from the first moment I
laid eyes on the man, although till that instant it had
never occurred to me that his intention was worse than
to exploit her wage-earning capacity.

"Katicha had had just time to scramble from the
cab and now stood beside me. While her father paid
the cab-driver, I took her by the hand firmly and
walked across the street to where in an open shop I saw
a crippled, elderly, evil-looking cobbler stooping and
tapping at his bench.

" 'See here, my old one,' I said, 'you live here, evidently. Tell me something, will you?'

"He looked at Katicha and me, surprised.

" '*What do the neighbors think of that house
yonder?*'

"He looked across the street at it, at our cab in front
of it, back at Katicha's fresh young face, at me with
an insulting appraising eye. And smiled.

"By my Stone Age ancestors! I was ready for the
man who, as I turned about, was coming angrily toward me, his hand outstretched to take Katicha's.

"I put the child behind me, and let him have it."

The narrator drew a deep breath and flung up her arms in a bold free gesture.

"Ah, never say that *all* memories lose their savor as the years roll by! I shall sink into my grave more satisfied with life because of the words that came to my lips in that hour. Thank heavens I am no fine-bred Aryan lady who dreads a scene! I made a scene there that it took the whole street to hold. Without boasting, I don't think the woman lives who could have made a worse one.

"But my opponent was not one to fear scenes. He too had days of pent-up exasperation to discharge. They exploded in my face in one wild blast of threats of blackmail, mixed with bellowed reminders that I had not a legal leg to stand on. The child was his, born in lawful marriage, with all the proper papers to attest it. If I interfered, I knew what the laws of France were about the rights of parents. *If I interfered* . . . ! He would not only have the law on me, he would blacken my reputation—end my career as a teacher. Could I deny that I had forced myself on him? Before a whole village full of witnesses I had insisted on traveling with him. How could I defend myself against charges of misconduct with him on the train? He would name the day and hour and minute of my misconduct, and there would be details. He went loudly into some of them. Finally if I knew so well what kind of house that was, and what sort of business his was, why had I so insisted on being taken to it? His leer as he said this last would have sickened to faintness any woman less infuriated than I. If I made a move against him he yelled, if I did not instantly take my hands off his daughter he would smirch my name till I was cast out into the gutter!

"All this in Basque, you must understand, for a crowd of low Marseilles idlers at once gathered around us and we had no mind to let them share in the dispute.

"Dispute!" Her voice was like the rich, deep clang of a great bell. "It was no mere dispute. It was a battle royal, a duel to the death, such as makes one forever greater to have fought. By heavens! to have been once wholly, madly angry like that and to have poured it all out in adequate words . . . It's like falling in love, or having a mystic vision. . . . One of the magnificent passages in life.

"Do you ask what happened? I faced him down. Why wouldn't I? I had all the right on my side, hadn't

I?—such epic right that a mouse could have strangled a tiger with it. Why should I fear his threats or so much as think of them? What did I do? I kept my eyes on his, my hand tightly around Katicha's wrist, my tongue molten with my opinion of him and my counter-threats of denunciation of him if he dared attack me then or afterward, and backed slowly down the street toward the corner where a trolley-line crossed it.

"He literally foamed with fury to see us escaping, the white flecks flying from his mouth with his curses. But it had all happened so rapidly and so violently he could not collect himself to think of any attack on me he dared undertake in broad daylight with a crowd of onlookers, especially as I grappled his eyes to mine with all the strength there was in me and took a fresh hold on vituperation with every breath I drew. No, he did not venture to touch me. But gods above! How he swore! And I answered him word for word.

"You've doubtless heard that our old language was set in its final form aeons ago, before even the Bronze Age, and that there are in it no words for modern objects, no names of metal tools, for instance. That is true. But evidently blood flowed hotly in human veins even before the use of metals was discovered. There may be no words in our vernacular for electricity or steel, but believe me, it has plenty of words for freeing the heart of wrath. We left none unused, that dastard Basque and I, as screaming at the tops of our lungs in our unintelligible tongue we moved down that sordid street, surrounded by that gaping crowd of Southern French loafers.

"Even after the frightened child and I were safely on the trolley car and slowly moving away, he continued to yell blood-curdling threats and imprecations after us, and I, leaning half my body over the railing of the back platform and boring my eyes into his, gave him as good as he sent."

She stopped the tocsin-like clanging of her voice to breathe, and in a moment went on in her ordinary tone: "I wanted, you see, to make a substantial impression on his imagination. Something that would last him! Even after the sound of my voice was out of his ears."

I said respectfully, "You did, I take it."

"Oh, yes, he never ventured to show his face here again. If he blackened my character, it never reached Itsasmendia, and so it didn't hurt me. I'd let him know that if he bothered Katicha or me again I'd tear France to pieces with public statements about what kind of father he was. No; the only difficulty I had after we left Marseilles was the regret of the Beheretche family over Katicha's nice new clothes left in her new valise in that cab. They never did get over my carelessness in not remembering to bring those back.

"But though he couldn't reach us, he had only a few years to wait. When Katicha was eighteen she fell in love. Her sweetheart was a good lad; it was a suitable match. Her grandparents had no objection. But it was her father who had the legal rights there. And you'd better believe he made full use of them. Certainly, he wrote, he would *not* give his consent to the marriage of Katicha to this fellow, or to any other. She could—his venomous grin shone through the letter—she could just wait the twelve years till she could marry without his consent.

"Here was a blow from an ax. And a sharp one. There was a great boiling-up of family councils, in which I earnestly participated. But they came to nothing. Of course, if there had been plenty of money and a friend at court to secure the services of a trustworthy lawyer, and stamped paper and evidence and proof, the case would have been fought out, and Katicha freed of such a father. But the French law is remarkably like that of other countries in that recourse to it is seldom safe for the poor and ignorant folk with no influential friends. All of us insignificant villagers shrank back at the thought of the possible—probable—certain—legal complications, ruinously expensive law-suits, and dirty mud-splashing which would follow any attempt to get the better of that bad man by process of law.

"There seemed to be nothing to do but wait. But the Basques are not a cool, self-possessed people who take to waiting with patience. The exasperated young lover put it to me many times with passion, that the right would surely be on their side if they simply made their home together openly, in the honesty of their innocent hearts. Remembering Katicha's father, I heartily agreed with the boy. But this revolutionary idea alarmed the orthodox grandparents and would have made the young couple outcasts in our pious commune. The young man grew dark and surly. Katicha drooped and pined and paled till it was a misery to see her.

"They had never said so, but in a dumb instinctive way all the Beheretche connection held me responsible for the enmity of the girl's father. True enough; in the strange way life's threads are twisted, I *was* responsible. As one is—you must have noticed this—somehow more responsible for the care of a dog one has saved from drowning than are the people who stood on the banks and did nothing. There was more than this slanting responsibility, the consequence of the mere facts of this particular case. There was—I felt it deeply—a far graver, more direct moral responsibility on my soul, because, having seen that earlier tragedy of frustrated love a generation ago, I could not avoid knowing exactly what wretchedness lay before those young people. *I* knew, I told myself, if nobody else did, what would happen to them if we older people allowed malignancy to stand between them and the fulfillment which was their right. Was I to stand passively by and see another man walk over the cliff to his death? Youth! Love! The very heavens should be moved—should they not? I asked myself—to protect those two sacred elements of life.

"There seemed to be, however, no heaven-mover available but me. The others were sunk in that dutiful submission to the will of God which I had so much admired in my earlier years. Well, what *could* be done? How could the most fervent ingenuity devise an escape out of the rat-trap into which the law and that abominable man had shut those two children? No civil marriage possible without the necessary papers and signatures. No church marriage either, without those. Any priest who tried that would involve himself and his parish and his bishop in ruinous controversy with the state officials. A blank wall in that direction. I was driven to consider more seriously the boy's rebellious notion of life in common, law or no law. Why indeed, for a mere meaningless formality, should those fresh young hearts wither? Twelve years to wait? Such healthy hearty organisms, meant for mating! It was not as though I did not know what those twelve years would mean to them. Had not the finger, writing on the wall, blazoned out before my youthful eyes the effects of such inhumanity? I saw again the burning eyes of that rebellious mourner at my first funeral in Itsasmendia.

"Yes, yes, all true enough. But by the time Katicha was eighteen I was nearly fifty years old. One does not live to that age without having guessed that tribal customs are based on something more than a senseless thirst for repression—that marriage laws have grown rigid precisely to resist a not uncommon thrust from within. Something occasionally happens to the ardent hearts of young lovers untrammeled by law, once they have had their way. What if this one should find the burdens and cares of a family too great a pressure without the stiffness of a legal code at his back? If there were no tie between him and his love save whatever he was pleased to admit, might he not after the usual experience of crying babies, poverty, sickness, strain, remember that he could, after all, just walk away from it all and start an easier life somewhere else? Katicha's grandparents were wise. To encourage an ignorant young girl to step into a situation with far more chances of unhappiness in it than she could divine —no, nobody had the right to take such responsibility.

"But one day, beating my head against all these dead walls, an idea came to me. One of my mother's cousins was a priest—and his parish was in Spain! Just across the frontier line, in a mountain pass. By the Spanish legal code he could marry whom he pleased in his own church, if all were in accordance with ecclesiastical law. Nothing would please him better, I surmised, than a chance to give a dig in the ribs to those laws of France which limit the right to bind in marriage to the secular

powers of the state. And a church marriage, legal or
not, would quiet wagging village tongues.

"So this is what we did. Both families went up over
the pass, bag and baggage, into the Spanish village, and
there we had a church wedding with every traditional
ceremony—green boughs strewn on the floor of the
church porch, flowers everywhere, chanted High Mass,
maid of honor, best man, the usual old woman at the
door with a basket of rose-petals to throw at the wed-
ded pair, and a little boy at hand to be the first person
the bride should kiss, to make sure that her first child
would be a son.

"Of course not a scrap of this was legally binding on
French citizens. But I'd figured that for a good boy as
Katicha's lover was, and a good Catholic, all that ceremony would make the necessary impression of stability
on his mind. I'd been so successful, you see, with the
impression I'd made on the mind of Katicha's father—
I quite fancied myself as a practitioner of the fine art
of making impressions—and of running other people's
lives for them."

She paused and looked down at her hands in a medi-
tative silence.

"Well—?" I inquired.

She answered in a neutral tone:

"They have had four children in the twelve years since then, all of them alive and well, and Katicha's thirtieth birthday being now near, the date is set for the legal ceremony in the mayor's office. There's never been the least doubt about the stability of that marriage."

Did she emphasize the word "stability"? If so I did not notice it, carried away as I was at the thought of her courage and devotion.

"Why, I think that's wonderful!" I breathed enthusiastically. "How proud you must be to know that such a thriving little family owes its very existence to your protection! One more of the happy memories you will take into your old age, one more service to . . ."

The sharpness of her interruption cut through my words as though they had been butter. She clove them to nothingness with one brief phrase: "It is the family of Jean-Pierre Gorena."

"*No!*" I cried explosively. I recoiled from her in incredulity. "You don't mean that—"

She turned an ironic dark eye on me and nodded.

I still could not believe I had understood her. "Not the Gorena family that *I* know!" I insisted. "Not my neighbors! Not that fisherman who passed here an hour ago!"

She nodded again, the curves of her mouth drooping, her eyes shadowed.

"Do you mean to say that he's not even *married* to that worthless nagging shrew—that all this time he has had the legal right to walk off and be—"

"Yes, the legal right," said his old teacher profoundly. "But he will never, never escape her."

"In heaven's name, why not?" I cried. "She makes life a perfect hell for him."

"Don't pretend to me," said my friend, "that at your age you have never observed that sensitive people are completely helpless before callous ones, conscientious ones before unscrupulous. I told you at the beginning, didn't I, that Jean-Pierre was a good boy who wanted to do the right thing? He still does. And Katicha has simply turned out to be her father's own daughter, a natural-born exploiter of others. Note well that never once did that possibility enter my mind as I goddessed from the machine. It is such wisdom as that, of course, which gives me the right to rearrange other people's lives for them."

She paused. I could think of nothing to say.

"You will now admit," she went on, looking at me gravely, "that you slightly overstate the case when you so poetically speak of that wonderful achievement of mine as another happy memory of service to others to take into my old age."

I could still less think of anything to say.

"And yet—" she asked it of the bright sky and kind life-giving sunshine—"what is one to do? Because some dogs kill sheep, should one stand coolly by without lifting a hand to pull a drowning puppy from the ditch?"

She got no answer from me to that question.

"Well, at any rate it will last me to my dying day as a riddle to puzzle over. But—will one's dying day perhaps be rather overcrowded with riddles?"

While I contemplated this one dumbly, she said with a laugh that was not of amusement, "One thing at least has been for some time quite clear to me. As far as her father is concerned, if he but knew it, the joke was by no means on him, that day in Marseilles."

# GOLD FROM ARGENTINA

P THE steep slope to Mendigaraya toiled an automobile, and this was remarkable, for Mendigaraya lies high in the Pyrenees, is geographically fifteen miles from a railroad, spiritually two centuries from the modern world, and does all of its business by ox-cart. The only contact with the twentieth century known to that region is through the occasional departure of one of the poorest boys, starved out, who emigrates to South America, and through the very infrequent return of one years later, either as a ragged failure or as a pot-bellied, well-to-do man in store clothes and suspenders, accompanied by a heathenish wife with a hat on her head. (Any Basque woman used to covering her sleek black hair with a mantilla would as soon go out on the street in her chemise as in a hat. And no Basque mountaineer, his lean, agile body sashed in red, ever gets enough to eat or can stop work long enough to acquire corpulence.)

Unless they come back to visit their old homes the emigrants are seldom heard of after their departure. Basques poor enough to be driven to emigrate can rarely read and write. Even if they could their families could not read their letters. For the most part they disappear forever, the strong, handsome young men despairing at the grinding narrowness of the lives before them, who pluck up courage to take the plunge, and, hiding their homesick panic under a pale bravado of gayety, set off down the long stony road leading to St. Jean-de-Luz and the railroad.

But of course one never knows; this car might be bringing a returned "American," as Basques who have lived in Argentina are always called. What other possible reason could an automobile have for coming to Mendigaraya? The little boys in blue bérets, playing *pelote* up against the wall of the church, halted their nimble sandaled feet and stared at the strange vehicle panting into the far end of the village street. The girls, drawing water at the fountain, stopped their chatter and turned their long, lustrous eyes toward it in wonder.

The automobile turned the one corner of the street and stopped short, stalling with a grunt of astonishment, for it found itself in an impasse, low, whitewashed, red-beamed houses before it, set thick all around a small public square of beaten earth, shaded by pollarded plane-trees. There was no way out between the houses, not even an alleyway. Mendigaraya is at the end of the road and does not mind admitting it.

The door of the car opened, and a man stepped out, instantly known, by all the Basque eyes looking at him, to be not a Basque. He had stiff leather shoes on his feet, and his stiff, wooden-legged gait was that of a city-dweller. He looked about him, saw that one of the houses announced by a faded sign that it was both the city hall and the post office, and stumping over to it, knocked on its door.

The elderly postmaster, who was also the town clerk and who had, like everybody else in town, been staring

Manuel Bidaranty, who, sixty-two years ago, at the age of nineteen, had gone to South America. Here was the record of his birth, his baptism, all the data about his securing his passport.

The lawyer pulled from his black leather portfolio a packet of documents, compared names, dates, ages. Evidently—he remarked after a time—evidently the same man.

He folded his documents together and returned them to his serviette, remarking that he had just received word from a lawyer in Buenos Aires that M. Bidaranty was dead.

How strange, thought the town clerk, to hear one of such a tribe as the Bidarantys called a *monsieur!*

The lawyer went on to say that, dying, M. Bidaranty had willed what property he had to his two sisters. Now that the identification was complete, there were only some legal formalities to be finished. They would take perhaps a month—perhaps two—possibly as long as three. Inheritances were long in getting themselves settled. And then he would transfer the property to the two heiresses.

The town clerk had listened to this, open-mouthed, his eyes wider and wilder with every breath he drew.

He now asked in a faint voice if it would be indiscreet to inquire whether M. Bidaranty had left much?

No, the lawyer told him, it would not be in the least indiscreet. No secret about it. Quite a tidy little sum. About three million dollars.

He reached for his hat and stepped toward the door.

The town clerk sat stricken, numb to his marrow.

"Good day," said the lawyer pleasantly, opening the door, "and many thanks for your assistance."

He stepped out.

The town clerk came to life with a convulsive shudder and cried after him in a cracked voice, "Did you say dollars? Or francs?"

"Dollars," said the lawyer, conversationally, and stepping into his car, disappeared.

The town clerk never was the same man again.

Mendigaraya reeled from the shock. The news flared up and down the narrow valley like fire in dry weeds, and in a twinkling burned away a number of false ideas about the Yturbe and Haratz families. Everybody saw now what he had not chanced to note before, that the Yturbes had great natural distinction of manner, and that the younger Haratz girls had wonderful hair and eyes. Everybody remembered what respected citizens they had always been, and there was a universal feeling among the better people of the town that it was not suitable for members of such good old families to be in menial positions. Generous friends, whose fathers had been the intimate friends of their fathers, rushed to help them out of their temporary difficulties. Before long one of the grandsons was taken into partnership by the village grocer. Three of the granddaughters, servant girls, were sought in marriage by sons of well-to-do farmers who worked their own land and owned many head of cattle. Another grandson, who had been stableboy for the doctor in the next town, the doctor who had once been almost elected to the Chamber of Deputies, was taken into the doctor's family on the most familiar terms and was already a great favorite with the doctor's marriageable daughter. An Yturbe boy! Think of it!

The two old ladies, now dressed in shining black silk presented to them by friendly neighbors, were removed from the earth-floored huts in which they had always lived and borne their numerous children, into salubrious new quarters in an elegantly furnished house, with sheets on the beds, wax flowers in glass bells on the mantelpieces, and actually—almost the only one in the village—a cast-iron two-holed cook-stove in the kitchen. Of course the bewildered, docile old women never did any cooking on the stove, the fire on the hearth being so much handier.

This house was thrown open to them in a burst of humanity by the only landed proprietor thereabouts, a wealthy Frenchman who owned four of the houses in town and had three farms to rent. He was on the point of settling, rent free, on one of his farms, a widowed daughter of Mme. Yturbe, when a sudden thought struck him, waking him up in the night, piercing to his vitals.

By dawn the next morning his son, a well-to-do horse-trader, as shrewd as himself, was dispatched down the road to St. Jean-de-Luz with instructions to see that lawyer in person and find out the truth about this wild story, which, after all, as the proprietor had suddenly remembered, rested on nothing more than the uncorroborated say-so of the town clerk, who, judging from the state of extreme agitation in which he had been found after the visit of the lawyer, might easily have misunderstood the whole business.

The horse-dealer left at six one morning. By nine, everybody in the village (with the natural exception of the Yturbe and Haratz families) knew why he had gone. They were all shuddering at the danger they had unwittingly been in and were thanking Providence that they had for a townsman so sagacious a person as the proprietor. During the two days of his absence the village went into a trance of suspended animation.

On the evening of his arrival the village notables assembled at his house to hear his report. It threw them into a veritable ague. He had not, it is true, been able to see the lawyer, who was away from his office and would not be back for a fortnight more. And, shrewd son of a worldly-wise Gallic father, he had been far too knowing to confide in a mere jackanapes of a lawyer's clerk. But he had heard—what had he not heard!

All St. Jean-de-Luz was talking of it. He had heard from everybody that the whole story was a hoax, an infamous practical joke. Jean Manuel Bidaranty had returned from South America years ago, a poor vagabond, like all the other Bidarantys, had earned a scanty living in a fishing-village farther up the coast, and when he died, had not left enough money to bury him. Everybody knew all the details of the true story—had heard in just which cemetery his poor wooden cross was to be found, had been told the full name of the fisher-

man who had employed him. Three million dollars
nothing! Of all the preposterous tales! Nobody but
backwoods simpletons would have believed for an instant such a preposterous story.

The assemblage of village notables, headed by the
almost-Deputy himself, who had gathered to hear the
news, turned with one accord to rush out and denounce
the wretched impostors. But the proprietor called them
back in an agonized voice. They had no more *proof* of
this last story than of the first. Suppose the Yturbes and
Haratz families were not wretched impostors at all, but
really valid heirs to three million dollars. It would not
do to be in too great haste. The story did sound madly
impossible, and thanks be to God and all the saints,
there was still time to draw back. But *suppose it should
be true!*

The group of notables glared upon each other with
tortured faces. Superior, upper-class people as they
were, they expected as a matter of course to dominate
any situation in which they found themselves and to
extract from it whatever profit there might be, naturally the due of the refined and cultivated. But this
situation—! Until the lawyer came back, what would
be safe for them to do? To *do?* How could they even

know what to feel, utterly at sea as they were, with no data on which an intelligent person could form a judgment? Were those Haratz girls really handsome, or were they common slatterns? Were the Yturbe boys promising lads or the scum of the earth? How could anybody know? Were ever human beings put into so hideous a situation as the townspeople of those two families?

Shut into this suspense, in the intolerable position of having nobody to blame, their nerves gave way, and they turned on each other. Before that first meeting had broken up, they had begun to quarrel fiercely, twitting each other with old scandals, raking up forgotten family skeletons, which, by the customary conspiracy of silence among gentry, had been kept dark lest the lower classes learn of them. Their exasperation found a real relief in this wrangling, which, after the fashion of wrangling, rose in intensity and fury from day to day. What else could do to fill those long slow days of waiting?

The apoplectic French proprietor, meeting Mme. Haratz in her black silk dress on the street, put up his hand to doff his hat to her, snatched it down again indignantly, put it up again falteringly, and glared upon her in an uncertainty so tragic that he felt something give way in his brain and fell to the ground in the first of the paralytic seizures which finally carried him off. People were as tense as fiddle strings. If wheels sounded in the street every one leaped to his window and was enraged to see that it was only the miller with an ox-cart loaded with bags of corn.

Even in their confusion, however, there was one thing which was almost at once obvious to them all. Whatever happened, they could prevent the others from exploiting those dumb ignorant peasants. They were revolted by each other's sordid calculations. Secretly, one by one, they went to warn the Yturbe and Haratz families. It was a Christian duty, they told Mme. Haratz, to let her know that the doctor's mother had died in an insane asylum and that the doctor often showed signs of the same malady, homicidal mania. Did Mme. Yturbe perhaps know that the proprietor of their house had been accused of poisoning his first wife? And did the Haratz girls know that the young men who had shown such mercenary haste in seeking them out after it was known they were heiresses were not all what they should be—were drunkards—thieves—had illegitimate families in other villages—had served

terms in prison—walked in their sleep? And had the
Yturbes happened to hear that it was the persecutions
of the grocer that had driven his former partner to
suicide?

To these revelations of the criminal, diseased, and
depraved character of their neighbors, the Yturbe and
Haratz families listened, open-mouthed, pale-cheeked,
panic-struck, credulous. They doubted not a word of
it. It fell in perfectly with their conception of life,
founded on tremulous notions of witchcraft and black
art. Never, never had they dreamed that the people
around them were so dangerous, so savage, so adroit—
but now that they knew it, it seemed quite under-
standable.

They held a council of their own, at night, behind
locked doors—cowering together, starting at every
sound, constantly sending one of the boys to make sure
no one was listening at the windows. What could they
do? How could they escape from the perils around
them? How could they, poor, ignorant, bewildered,
helpless folk as they were, hold their own against these
upper-class, highly educated assassins, crooks, robbers,
and maniacs who surrounded them, as they had all seen
a flock of sheep surrounded by wolves?

No idea of resistance crossed their minds. Never in the memory of man had any one of them been able to defend himself against property-owners, who could read and write and cipher, and knew how to get the law on you if you didn't do as they wished. Open resistance would not have the faintest shadow of success. And even if fighting could have saved them, there was not a drop of fighting blood in the lot of them.

But—like an inspiration it came to them—there are other ways of escape for creatures who dare not fight. With a huddled, sheeplike rush, once the idea was conceived, they made their plans. The night was a dark one. There were plenty of strong arms to carry the children. They could be far, far on their way before dawn. For at least twenty-four hours, perhaps longer, no one could guess where to look for them. And it would take a good day, after that, to find them. Fifteen miles, while long and hard for the soft feet of well-to-do folk, does not seem far to people used to work hard for their living. And it was all downhill to St. Jean-de-Luz.

Four days later the son of the proprietor once more came back from a trip to St. Jean-de-Luz. He was gray with fury. They had gone. The whole tribe. To Buenos

Aires. To where Jean Manuel had lived. They had
found the lawyer just returned to his office, and had
asked him, so he said, if they had the right to go? If
there was money enough to pay for their tickets? If
any one could get the law on them if they did go? The
lawyer had bought their tickets for them and helped
them get off. After all, why not, he had said impu-
dently to the man from Mendigaraya, if that was what
they wanted?

No, it had not been a hoax about the money. All
solid fact. Just as the lawyer had said at first. Incredible. True.

## THE COURSE OF TRUE LOVE

 "I NEVER did have any luck—but once," said the school-teacher, when somebody mentioned match-making, "trying to arrange young people's love-affairs for them. Love-affairs are like children—seem to do better for a lot of letting alone."

"What was the once?" I asked.

"I call it once," she said, smiling to herself, "but when it happened it seemed like many times—like twice, at least. Just when I thought it was all over and I was through with it, to have to . . ."

"Was it here?"

197

"Well, part of it. I told you it was complicated. Yet it started like water running downhill or the sun rising in the morning—with sweethearts who were boy and girl on adjoining farms, always a convenient marriage for farmers' children to make. They were of suitable age, both pure-blooded Basques as sound as nuts, and everybody approved of their marrying. They weren't perhaps exactly formally engaged, but neither of them had ever looked at anybody else; Pedro's parents were thinking which room to vacate for the young people, and Emiliana had begun to get her household linen ready.

"People thought no more about it than they did of the wheat ripening in the fields. Why wouldn't it ripen, planted in good earth, with the sun shining down on it? Pedro and Emiliana, endlessly talking to each other on a corner of the *place* on market days, always meeting each other at the door of the church after Mass and strolling slowly back to Etcheonda (that was the name of Emiliana's home), or dancing lightfootedly together at a wedding or christening party—to us, their elders, they were indistinguishable from a good wheat field following its natural course of turning golden in the sun of a good summer.

"That was all we knew about it. If I learned anything from that experience—and I did learn a good deal—it taught me sharply that men and women are never like wheat-stalks or anything else that's simple and vegetable. They are always human beings, complicated, incalculable.

"Into our town one fine day in May there came an automobile, one of the first of those infernal machines ever seen here, bringing people who were perfectly in their right place in a noisy, expensive, bad-smelling machine. If there's one thing I detest more than an automobile it's a Basque who's gone Aryan. Of course the Basque country is very poor, and our Basque boys can't all stay here. Some of them must be sacrificed to go off to Argentina and get rich. But most of those who do have proved that such a fate needn't necessarily turn them into either Americans or Europeans! In that car sat one who had turned into I don't know what. A Basque born and brought up in Zurrugne till he was sixteen. I remembered him well at that age, a narrow-hipped, supple, bright-eyed boy, one of our best *pelote* players. I was in *la place* the day they arrived and was one of the first to see him, but if he hadn't called out to me, giving his name, I'd never have recognized him,

poor thing! A great white waistcoat stuffed full of
flabby paunch hung down on thick thighs as he sat
there in his Hispano-Suiza; wrinkled pouches of skin
under his eyes hung down on clay-colored cheeks.
Could that be Ferdinand Lamberbaita! And such a
wife and daughter as he had for his sins! Painted, hat-
ted women in gaudy-colored dresses, with dreadful little humped, misshapen French or American feet (I
never did learn whether his wife was North American
or French) in high-heeled slippers.

"They were making their first trip to Europe, it
seemed, and when they got as far as Biarritz he had
decided to stop a day before they went on for a
motor tour in Spain, and run up to Zurrugne to show
his wife and daughter his old home village—'not
changed at all,' he cried, looking around him; 'but
nothing, nothing, nothing at all is different!'

"They got out of the car and we walked across the
square, his crippled women hobbling beside us in their
dreadful shoes. He kept exclaiming to me, turning his
head around and around. 'But it's positively as if I had
never gone away! You look just as you did when you
used to scare the life out of us over the rule for the
agreement in number and gender of past participles.

The cypresses in the graveyard are no taller, the plane-trees here in *la place* haven't a leaf more or less! The *pelote* court—I know every inch of that end wall! And those battered old benches for spectators! My God, there are boys playing there this minute—look like the very same ones who used to play with me!'

"That's what he saw. What his wife saw I can't imagine—probably nothing more than that her satin slippers were getting dusty. She never seemed to be aware of anything more than that sort of thing. I imagine she must have come from the lowest of the poor, to begin with, she was so crazy about her fine clothes. What his daughter saw was plain from the first, Pedro Elissagaray playing *pelote*. He was not one of our best players ever—too lazy to drive himself hard enough to get the lungs for a long match. But he was one of the most ornamental. And *pelote* is one of the most becoming games a good-looking, supple young man can play.

" 'No, I don't believe I'll go into the church,' she said coolly to her father. 'I can survive if I don't see the font where you were baptized. I'll just sit here awhile and watch this game.'

"I didn't think it decent to leave a girl alone on the

benches at the *fronton*—the boys weren't playing, only practicing for the next match; so there weren't any other spectators. But it was no affair of mine. And they evidently had given up trying to make her do anything but what she wanted. So I just said good-by to them at the church door and went my way, very sorry for a Basque who looked like that and had such women-folks.

"I heard the next day from everybody—for, of course, everybody made it his business to walk by the *fronton* or to watch from behind closed shutters—that the bold, ill-bred girl never took her eyes from Pedro's face, and when her father and mother came out she called them over to watch too. And then Pedro some-how had stopped playing and was talking to them, and then they took him off to the inn, where they all drank more Izarra than was good for them and M. Lambert (that was the absurd way he had clipped off his good Basque name) bragged about what a grand *pelote* player he had been in his youth. Pedro had no head for alcohol, and the innkeeper's wife, who naturally kept track of all they said, told me that in no time he was playing the fool, making up to the daughter and being respectful to the parents. It ended by their taking him off right as he was, down back to Biarritz with them. Pedro had never been in an automobile before, and you'd better believe he didn't refuse when they invited him.

"We never dreamed, of course—that being the first American-brought-up daughter we had ever seen—that anything would come of it except a headache for Pedro. They were, you'll remember, to leave the next day for that motor trip in Spain. But they didn't. Mlle. Lambert it was who had the headache—or toe ache—something which made her, she said, in no condition for travel. So they stayed on in Biarritz, and Pedro most of the time with them. He hardly came home at all, and when he did he looked and acted like somebody who's taken too much laughing-gas at the dentist's. As if he could scarcely make out to see Zurrugne at all any more. Neither Zurrugne, nor his family, nor Emiliana. Every time he came he brought some new piece of news more fantastic than the others: M. Lambert was crazy about his *pelote* game, was going to take him back to Argentina to play *pelote* there, where a good player made more money in a year than the whole of Zurrugne since the days of living in caves! Then that he was playing often now on the stylish *fronton* at Biarritz with the Lambert family looking on, and a big banknote every time he made a specially good showing. Then that he was learning to dance, not those Basque dances that were just acrobatics for men, but real French dances, and with Mlle. Lambert in his arms spent half of every night on the ballroom floor of the costliest hotel in Biarritz. And then—of course—what was to have been expected, only we could not imagine such a thing, Mlle. Lambert was mad over him, wanted to marry him, and her parents could refuse her nothing. But he—he said this to a group of older people one evening on *la place*—he, of course, felt himself bound to Emiliana, whose heart would be broken and whose life laid waste if he took advantage of this golden opportunity. Yes, said his parents steadfastly, that was true.

"But Emiliana released him as soon as this speech of his reached her, which you may be sure it did in less time than a magpie would take to fly from *la place* to Etcheonda. She sent for me—I'd had both her and Pedro in my class, of course—and very pale and tearful and noble and dignified, bade me tell Pedro that she would not for anything in the world stand between him and good fortune, that she would never forgive herself if she did, that she knew her duty when she

saw it and gave him back his troth. I remember thinking—what strange ideas old maids have!—that she
was one of the most heroic creatures I'd ever heard of,
thus to give up her lover for his own sake to another
woman. Yes, I learned a thing or two out of that story.

"Of course I didn't tell Pedro anything. I was so
furious with him I'd have slapped his face if I'd met
him. I passed it on to him through some cousins of his,
and he vanished almost completely—to Biarritz.

"This had been going on so long that there was now
only a fortnight before the end of the school year. I
never put in a worse two weeks. Like all Basques I am
an *impulsive*, given to acting violently when I feel
violently. But here was something that condemned me,
almost as if I were an Anglo-Saxon, into feeling violently without acting at all. I couldn't sleep for rage,
for pity, for indignation. Emiliana's desolate white
face was constantly before me, replaced by Pedro's
complacent smirk. Was he to be allowed to succeed in
this infamy, this treason to everything there was in him
of any value—his love, his Basque inheritance? Wasn't
there any way of bringing him back to that splendid
girl at Etcheonda? How stone- and stock-like we had
all stood by, not raising a hand to prevent this misery!

As I saw Emiliana going back and forth to market, tall and stately under her head-basket, I used to feel such a fury of compassion and anger that I was stiff with it.

"On the last day of school Pedro happened to come back to Zurrugne for one of his rare short visits to his parents, and that settled the matter for me. I could have endured perhaps his screaming yellow leather shoes, perhaps even his French clothes and his straw hat. But he had grown a little mustache! A Basque with hair on his face like a Frenchman! That just pushed me over the edge.

"Of course, there always is a way out when you feel violently enough. That night again I did not sleep, but before morning I had thought of two ways out. And the next day I went down to stay at Biarritz for a while myself. A poor school-teacher at Biarritz? Expensive, luxurious, fashionable resort of millionaires? Bah! It's simply a part of purse-proud European insolence to forget that Biarritz is also—in the old quarter —just another Basque town. I had an aunt and a cousin living there, in the grocery business, and I invited myself to make them a visit.

"But the grand promenades and the *chic* beach and the costly shops and the glittering streets of the expensive quarters are open to anybody, even poor school-teachers, and it wasn't long before, after a few days of running after Pedro, I succeeded in running into him. At first he looked a little surprised at my friendliness, but soon—I could see the thought coming into his eyes as clearly as I used to see plans for some school naughtiness come into his little-boy face—he thought to himself, 'Oh, yes, of course, all my poverty-stricken old acquaintances who never paid much attention to me before will be making up to me now I am going to marry a millionaire's daughter and play *pelote* in Buenos Aires.' He began to twist one end of his little mustache and to be condescending to his poor shabby old school-teacher.

"But he stopped that soon enough. After a day or so, meeting him here and there and smiling on him like any doting aunt, I brought out little by little the first of my plans. I suggested to him lightly—one day one idea, the next day another—that he was, after all, an inexperienced boy, with a tendency to think things were just what they seemed, which they almost never were. What, when it came down to facts, did anybody know so much about these Lamberts? Perhaps they didn't have any real money in spite of all they were throwing away here. Maybe, for instance, they had their property in one of those silver mines that went bust from one day to the next, leaving their owners and everybody connected with them loaded with debt. That, for all he knew, they might be running up huge bills here at the hotel. And so forth and so on.

"He looked sober enough after a time, my Pedro, and let his French mustache alone. If I'd had one I'd have twirled it all right.

"But that was no go. He had much more capacity for directing his grabbing than I'd given him credit for. He went right to the hotel management and by a little tipping (with Lambert money, of course) found out their bills were paid on the dot and big tips thrown around like pebbles. And one day when M. Lambert was talking business with his lawyer, down from Paris, Pedro contrived to sit there in the room listening, and learned that the Lambert fortune, solidly distributed in the best securities, was ten times bigger than he'd dared to dream. He told me all this the next time we met, just to reassure an old friend anxious about him. I had to smile and look pleased and congratulate him. I all but dropped dead of apoplexy.

"So then, hoping that Emiliana wouldn't have

no man—ignorant, dumb, weak peasant that he is—to cope with that girl, nor to inherit that fortune. He'd lose it for them in no time. What they really are looking for, of course, now they are back in France with all those millions, is somebody who could introduce them to Society and secure for them the position which millions deserve.'

"Yes, M. le Député and his son quite caught my point, nodding and looking thoughtfully down at their beautifully cut trousers that probably weren't yet paid for. A day or so after this, as I stood talking with them for a moment, I saw Pedro and Mlle. Lambert approaching on the other side of the street, he in all the *chic* clothes money could buy, she in one of her outrageous get-ups that revealed to any woman's eye what a cheap, hard-boiled, coarse creature she was at heart. They might have passed the dowdy old school-teacher from Pedro's home town without seeing her, but noting that I was chatting to M. le Député and his fashionably notorious son, they gave me the kind little nod of people who feel superior and want to show they don't.

" 'Oh, you know them personally?' exclaimed Gaudreau *père* after they'd passed. Gaudreau *fils* had lifted his heavy white night-club eyelids enough to watch her gaudy figure as she went on down the street.

"'I knew that millionaire,' said I, 'when he was Ferdinand Lamberbaita, with only one pair of *espadrilles* to his name and glad of an extra hunk of *arto* for his supper of a night.' And then I asked them, with the impulsiveness that naturally comes with an idea newly popped into your head, 'See here, wouldn't you be interested in meeting them, M. le Député? Of course I know they are only an undistinguished new-rich couple. But I suppose a statesman feels it his duty to meet all kinds of people.'

"Well," said the school-teacher with a long breath, "I needn't take up your time telling what you know already—the quick hash that was made of the bungling village boy by that experienced, money-famished Casino frequenter. Pedro had never had but one sweetheart, and she was an honest girl. Gaudreau *fils* knew all there is to know about women—one kind of woman —in five languages. A girl with ordinary decent instincts couldn't have endured him in the room with her. But he was—with his slick manners and social prestige and bad reputation—exactly the man to impress such a woman as that Mlle. Lambert.

"In fact it went so rapidly and so conclusively—

very much like the snap of a large, well-oiled steel trap—that in no time I was thanking my aunt and my cousin for their hospitality, such as it was, and was buying my third-class ticket back to St. Jean Pied-de-Port.

"My cheerfulness about what I'd done lasted me till I got off the train and was trudging up the street to the corner where the diligence to Zurrugne passes. But you know how it is in travel; long before your body gets to where you're going, your mind has arrived and is walking around looking at things. As I sat on my satchel on the sidewalk there in St. Jean I really was at Zurrugne and beyond, on my way up to Etche-onda, to tell Emiliana that her lover would soon be back. I even knew the day and hour to announce, for on my way to the station at Biarritz I had met him, loitering idly, pale and dispirited. On seeing me joy-fully starting for home, blessed home, full of honest people with hearts in their breasts, he had burst out in a sudden sullen desperation, 'I'm going home too. I'm sick and tired of it all down here. I won't wait a day longer. Tell my folks—and Emiliana—will you? —that I'll be back tomorrow on the afternoon dili-gence.'

"Yes, I knew that he would be along after me in a mere twenty-four hours, but waiting there at St. Jean I had a strange difficulty in thinking how to announce this to Emiliana. My imagination walked me easily up the road towards Etcheonda, but every time I actually approached the house and would soon have to see the girl and tell her—her whom I'd last seen proud and pale and desolate—my imagination balked and stood still. Not a word could I find in my head to tell her that her lover was returning to her, not a tone of my voice could I find that would fit the news that she was again to be favored with the attentions of a worthless, fickle, shallow-hearted, mercenary fellow.

"No, what came bursting up explosively into my mind was not a joyful cry, 'Emiliana! Your lover is returning to you! Smile and be glad!' but a savage 'Emiliana! That trash is on his way back to pick you up from where he dropped you. Have nothing to do with such a cheap piece of goods. Go into a convent and be a nun rather than marry the man you love, since now you know what manner of dog he is!'

"But—you will be asking—if I felt that way, why in the world had I cut myself into little bits to prevent Pedro's marrying that outlander and to make him re-

turn to Emiliana? The point is that I hadn't felt so till that moment. I had been so angrily occupied with punishing Pedro that there had been no fiber in my brain left for considering Emiliana's position, putting myself in her place. I saw that now. And I wasn't ashamed of it, either. Nothing can be accomplished by anybody who is thinking of two things at once. Nor am I an amiable person, ashamed of having been wholly indignant and revengeful. I abominate amiability. It is only another name for indifference. And one might as well lie rotting in his grave and be done with it as be indifferent. No, I was not ashamed, but, I must admit, rather disconcerted to find my thoughts once more lava, only flowing out of the volcano in quite another direction. Just as I had relaxed and settled back to rest a little after a period of wildly intense effort, here was another effort to be made, no less intense.

"The diligence came along and I climbed in, my mind rushing from one possibility to another—this time not for preventing Pedro's leaving Emiliana but for preventing her from seeing him when he returned. For I knew as soon as I thought of her that my only hope was to keep that fond girl from laying eyes on Pedro, at least for the time being. Being what she was

—that pale face of heroic renunciation!—one glimpse of her lover, repentant and despairing, would be enough. She would fall into his arms with but one thought—to console him. I knew, I told myself, the heart of womankind enough to foresee that. To tell you the truth, I'd astonished myself considerably by being so weak as to be very sorry for Pedro as I'd left him, hurt and bewildered and broken.

"But how ever in the world could I—could anybody—keep Emiliana from seeing him? She was never anywhere but at home, and he would be returning in just twenty-four hours by the very same diligence in which I now slowly lumbered my way up the road.

"I couldn't even number over to you all the crazy plans I thought of in that ride. I would invite her to go over the frontier with me to Spain, to visit some Spanish-Basque relations. I would work on her religious fervor to make a retreat in a convent. I would tell her that Pedro had contracted a dreadful disease. I would engage her as help for me and never let her out of my sight. I would this and I would that. The diligence arrived at Zurrugne and I climbed down and went home, still in a trance. But before I fell asleep I knew there was really only one thing to do, to make

an alliance with Emiliana's mother and contrive something with her help.

"When I did fall asleep I fell hard and far. I was really worn out by all that passionate feeling, not to speak of the fact that in Biarritz I'd been sleeping on a narrow sofa in the dining-room, my aunt not having a spare room, and my own bed felt like a foretaste of Paradise.

"When I woke up the sun was high and I heard the morning diligence lumbering by. It must be nearly ten, I thought, and sleepily aroused myself to dress and get a bit of breakfast. There was no need for haste, of course, and I took my time. Along about noon as I started up the road towards Etcheonda, I felt quite restored by sleep and being once more in decent footgear.

"Nobody was in sight as I toiled up the steep slope towards the house, and nobody visible as I stood at the door. I knocked and called. No answer. I looked in. Nobody there but the cat dozing on the window sill.

"Harvest season, I remembered. They were all probably out in the fields with their sickles. But they'd soon be home for the midday meal. I went around the house. There was a sort of terrace built up there, and I thought

217

I'd sit down to wait on the bench by the door, which commanded a fine view. And what, far down in the field at the foot of the hill, was the fine view that met my eyes—Emiliana embracing Pedro and being embraced by him with a fervor beyond anything!

"I fell backwards upon the bench. 'Not possible!' I shouted at the top of my voice. But it was possible. There was no mistaking Emiliana's tall, splendid figure, although it was no longer stately, but vibrant and as charged with electricity as a bolt of lightning. She drew herself now from Pedro's arms, held him at arm's length to gaze upon him, and once more flung herself into his embrace with an ecstasy of emotion that crackled all around me on the terrace, far away and tiny as the figures of the lovers were. Still enlaced in each other's arms, they moved back along the path as it wound into the woods and vanished from my sight.

"So I was too late. Pedro had changed his mind and come in by the morning diligence. And while I dressed at my leisure and ate breakfast, he had flung off his nightmare city clothes, had changed back to shirt, cotton trousers, sash, *espadrilles*, and béret—and had leaped up the hill to Etcheonda to find the constant heart that awaited him.

"I tried in a stunned, dumb kind of way to think what I now ought to do, and decided that the only decent thing left was to keep a shut mouth.

"I soon had occasion to do so, for Emiliana's mother now emerged from the house, very much surprised to see me. After the greetings were over and her explanation of how she had been in the barn doctoring a sick sheep, my eyes strayed to the two lovers emerging from the trees as their path wound upward and lay for a loop outside the forest across a slope of pasture.

"Emiliana's head was on Pedro's shoulder now, his arm evidently supporting her, his béret-covered dark head bent tenderly over hers.

"The mother's eyes followed mine. She smiled happily. 'Yes, isn't it wonderful,' she said, 'how God makes everything turn out right in the end for those who have faith. After all our anxiety for our dear girl!' I nodded.

"She went on, 'We just decided half an hour ago when the wedding would be. They've been down to announce it to my husband. It's set for a fortnight from today. We hope you will be one of the family party and sit at the table with the kindred.' I nodded.

"She looked down the hill again. But now, following the windings of the upward-bearing path, they had disappeared once more. 'I shall never repine again at any trial God sends,' she said devoutly. 'All that trouble and sorrow, it just cracked Emiliana's child-heart open so that it could let in real love. She used to be so cool and quiet, I almost feared that she had no vocation for marriage.'

"I gathered there was no doubt about that now.

"My silence perhaps made her feel that she was being rather emotional, for she now said briskly, 'And of course, it's a great satisfaction to Emiliana's father that his farm lies next to Etcheonda. It will be so much easier to plan the farm work that way.'

"What could I do but nod again? What was there to say?

"She decided to change the subject and sat down by me. 'You've been visiting your Aunt Marie, haven't you? How did you find them all? Well, I hope.'

"But I never answered that polite question. For now the lovers emerged from the trees just below the terrace, close to me. They looked up, their cheeks glowing, their eyes brilliant, a tableau of young love triumphant. They saw us sitting there and waved their hands gayly

to us. And—you probably guessed this at once—it was
not Pedro at all who had his arm around Emiliana.
It was Paulino Arainty, whose farm lay next to
Etcheonda on the other side."

# THE MAJESTY OF THE LAW

**T**HIS is the story of the great Basque witchcraft trial of the early seventeenth century as it was told to me in the twentieth. It must be, I suppose, part of the records of French courts, written down on parchment somewhere in legal language. And there is an ancient book in which the august Counselor of the Parliament of Bordeaux has set down in archaic French his own version of what he did and what happened to him in the summer of 1609. I tell it as it came to me in Itsasmendia, bit by bit, from the talk of people whose ancestors lived through it.

Much of the color and many of the traditional details came in chance passing mention of this or that by the grocer (also the maker of *espadrilles*) of the village, by the fisherman who supplied us with fish, by our sewing-woman (very proud, she was, that Dominica Dargaineratz was one of her great-great-grandmothers), and by a young farmer neighbor, part of whose sheep pastured on the slopes of La Rhune, the bodeful bald mountain, on whose summit the witches gathered for their worship of Jaun Gorri, the Red Lord. Naturally, the most connected version came from the doctor and the school-teacher, both intensively Basque. From them, too, came all of the historical background for that wild summer season, three centuries ago.

Of that historical background I had been as ignorant as possible. I had had in my life quite other things than sorcery to think about, and knew scarcely more than that a belief in witchcraft had been one of the superstitions of the past. To me, as to most other half-informed Americans (especially since Puritan-baiting has been in fashion), witchcraft mania suggested mostly Salem, Massachusetts. Now that for the first time I put my mind on the subject I discovered that I harbored the idea—if you can call a vague impression an idea—that our own flare-up of witch hunting was a part of the objectionable Puritan attitude towards life, could be laid to the vicious tendencies of those repressed Pilgrim Fathers. It was news to me that our affair at Salem had been the merest side-ripple of a tidal wave. Listening open-mouthed with astonishment to my Basque informants, I soon began hastily to throw up mental defenses of incredulity before their horrible pictures. They certainly must be laying it on too thick, in those descriptions of the insensate delusions of England and Europe during four centuries of obsession. Privately I thought they were exaggerating in their usual Basque pride at not belonging to our race, in their characteristic belief that this long bloody insanity was only another one of the consequences of the general Aryan inability to create a tolerable manner of living.

I did not tell my Basque friends what was in my mind as I listened to their account of how hysterically Europe and England had writhed in the terror of sorcery trials; but the first time I went up to Paris that summer, I gave myself the trouble of going to the National Library to consult some reliable historians.

I wanted to see if there were any historical basis whatever for their tales of thousands and thousands of
human beings done dreadfully to death, century after
century, as condemned sorcerers.

Any historian who may have read so far has certainly been astonished that I could have been so ignorant, and is probably now smiling in amusement at
the thought of my recoil from what lay waiting for me
in the records of the past at the great Paris library.
And indeed I was staggered to find that my Basques,
far from exaggerating, did not know the half of what
took place during the recurrent witchcraft scares which
from the year 1200 on submerged Europe from Scot-
land to Sicily, driving into murderous frenzies of
hysteric panic Anglo-Saxons, Germans, Scandinavians,
Celts, Latins—everybody.

Really *every*body? Well, read on and see.

In those records of the past life of Europe I saw the
mania grow from a spasmodic seizure here and there
into a long, incredible nightmare. I had never dreamed
that for three centuries all "civilized" European gov-
ernments had a regular department of jurisdiction
given over to the trying of witches. I was shocked to
find the procedure against sorcery as accepted a part

226

of legal lore as our legal procedure against housebreakers, in the hands of carefully trained lawyers and learned judges, one of whom claimed proudly as his great right to honor that he had condemned to death for sorcery more than ten thousand persons in the course of his life. Throughout two centuries, throughout three centuries, until well into the eighteenth century, those cultivated, studious Renaissance Europeans put their heads together to elaborate a horrific code of witchcraft practice. It filled large volumes, it had traditions and precedents and special rulings which, exactly like our present legal practice, were docilely learned by each succeeding generation of ambitious teachable young lawyers and practiced by them without a qualm of doubt.

As I read on and on in these inconceivable records I continually had the illusion that I must be in a bad dream; that—frightful as are the mistakes continually committed by our poor race—it really was not to be believed that human beings could have lost their heads so utterly, that in all those thousands of men and women in those three centuries, there were none with ordinary sense, and ordinary honesty and ordinary courage enough to protest. The hysteria of madness and cruelty and fear rose from the pages of the books I was reading like a poison gas. Those careful detailed accounts of the weighing of evidence and the cross questioning of witnesses—I looked down with a dizzy sickness into the black depths of their deliberate measured lunacy. I was continually raising my eyes to refresh myself, as by a gulp of fresh air, by the sight of the usual frowsy serious inelegant students bent over their books all about me in the reading room of the Bibliothèque Nationale.

Back again in Itsasmendia, the next week, I listened with fewer inward protests to my Basque friends, as they asked me, "Do you wonder that we are not dazzled by a civilization that produces that sort of thing? Do you wonder that we do not have for European subtlety, complexity, art, sophistication—European culture, in short—the same whole-hearted admiration which Europeans have? Our people have seen the Aryans' pride in learning lose them tragically in miseries out of which any honest child could find the way by instinct."

Did I say that all this horrid intellectual elaboration of witchcraft procedure, this creation of a flawless technique for producing hysteria, went without a single

protest? What is this story I am now beginning? It is
the story of what happened when the homespun primitive Basque country of poor farmers and beggarly
fishermen was invaded by Europe, draped in all its
ponderous legal lore, dignified in its rich prestige, its
unquestioned authority, with that European certainty
—the most marked characteristic of Europe to this
very day—that whatever Europe does is the absolute
last word in civilized procedure.

## II

That summer, three hundred odd years ago, began
apparently like all other Basque summers since the
beginning of time, by the exodus of all the able-bodied
men near the coast—off to the fishing banks of Newfoundland. Yes, they tell you, since the beginning of
time, not at all since 1492. All Basques know that they
did not wait for Christopher Columbus to discover another continent and extra good fishing grounds, but
that from the earliest days as now, Basque fishing ships
sailed out from Basque harbors bound for the Banks.
Indeed, any Basque will inform you of the very year
and day when Christopher Columbus, an obscure
mariner, happened to talk with two Basque sailors and

learned from them of the continent which he was later to present to the world as his own invention.

At any rate there is no doubt that for many centuries a fleet of small Basque fishing vessels have set sail from home in the spring and have not returned till the autumn. Nor is there any doubt that the men from Itsasmendia have always, just as they do now, gone up to a very old small massive chapel, half sunk in the earth, on the top of the cliff above Itsasmendia port, to say their prayers and receive a last blessing before they set the prows of their ships to the west. They said good-by to their families, each one in his own home, and then, all together, down to the lamest old man and tiniest baby, they trooped up to the Chapel of St. Nicholas. The women and children and the old men, all those who were to stay at home, did not enter. They knelt on the ground on the sea side of the old building. When the men came out from the chapel, after they had received their blessing and had prayed before the altar, they were already on their way. Two by two, they tramped down the winding path cut in the face of the cliff, took ship and were off—the prayers of those still kneeling beside the chapel floating above the ships like a bright invisible cloud of benediction. Many of those left remained on their knees for hours till—strain their eyes as they might—there was nothing left before them but the empty sea.

All summer long the women returned there singly to pray, their eyes on the sea which might at that moment be the grave of the man for whom their prayers were being said. As autumn approached, as the time neared when the fleet might be expected back, there was no hour, day or night, when there was not a watcher on the cliff beside the chapel flinging her heart out over the ocean. There was always some one here to see the first sail on the horizon, to run in to the bell tower of the chapel, and catching the bell-rope, to make the old bell turn head over heels, as it clanged out the news. What a moment in their lives, that first crazy shout from the bell of St. Nicholas, like no other voice of the year, rung at no other time. In every house and wood and field and pasture, they stopped to listen to it, resounding from the cliff.

Every one, from the old man making faggots in the distant copse to the little girl playing with her dolls, dropped what he was doing, turned in his tracks and made for the chapel. Here for centuries, year by year, came every one who could walk, watching the boats skim in over the ocean, trying to recognize them as they came. That little spot of earth is soaked with the tears of those whose boat was missing, is worn with the kneeling of those who, recognizing their own, prostrated themselves in thanksgiving. Here they stood, centuries ago, and here they still stand, as the tramp of the men's feet begins to mount the cliff. The bell stops its clanging. In the silence the firm tread of the men sounds on the rocky path. Around the point of rock like an incoming ocean tide they come, the bronzed, blue-jerseyed, deep-sea fishermen.

A great breath like a sigh goes up from the waiting crowd. But no words yet. No cries, no greetings. The first welcome is from God. The men march into the low dark chapel, open only on those two days of the year, and sink to their knees. Those who have waited press in after them, women with babies, little children holding each other by the hand, old men limping and bent. The priest's voice rises, the heads are bent, all those hearts swell and beat in joy, in misery . . . for there are always empty places in the ranks of the returned. It is a service of thanksgiving for the living, of remembrance for the dead. At the end silence, an instant's silence, and then the clanging of the bell as they rise from their knees and turn at last to each other.

So the return of the fishermen has been for more centuries than man can count . . . always the same except once . . . just once. Yet that year of 1609 when they went away in the spring, everything seemed exactly as usual. Life seemed as empty as the sea, after their departure, as it always did. There was not the slightest thread of communication in those days. When the boats dropped below the horizon they might have dropped into the black pit for all that was known of them by the people at home. For interminable months of every year the women and children lived in this void, did the work of men in the fields, tended the herds of cattle and sheep, kept the machinery of life moving, endured their loneliness as best they could and lay awake at night to wonder what was happening on the other side of the world.

These unnaturally lonely summers were hard for the Basque women left far too much to themselves, with far too great burdens of responsibilities, moral and material. Like all austere ways of life it was a magnificent school for the strong, a tragic strain for the weak and immature. All nerves were more or less taut, and there were often occasional cases of hysteria and temporary mental unbalance during those months.

Perhaps some such case was the beginning of this story. Or perhaps only that year had a report of those peculiar Basque habits penetrated to the outer world, and masculine European eyes found very suspicious the spectacle of mere women carrying on masterfully the life of a people. It may have seemed to those European men, used to shut-in, dependent, and passive women, that nothing but sorcery could explain the abnormal force of character of the bold active Basque matrons and girls, living without fear in the widely separated Basque farmhouses; for Basques, unlike the Aryans around them, have never been a village-folk. Each family lives apart on its own harsh, rocky and dearly loved bit of land.

Possibly there was not even so much reason in the affair as this. It may merely have been that the region around Bordeaux and to the north had been bled white by long years of witchcraft trials and that the Bordeaux judges, like any active energetic professional men, were looking for new fields of usefulness. All that I could learn about the beginning of that nightmare summer was that a report had been made to the Bordeaux

Courts setting forth that the Basque women were getting out of hand. One of the phrases in that report has been handed down verbatim in oral tradition and was often quoted to me . . . "the country of the Basques stands thick in apple trees and the women are so many Eves who have eaten of the forbidden fruit of the tree of knowledge."

Whatever started the affair, all the quiet country along the Bay of Biscay from Biarritz to Hendaye was, early in June of 1609, startled by the news of the installation at the St. Jean-de-Luz Court House of a group of august lawyers and judges from the Bordeaux Courts for Sorcery. The untraveled rustics of the region looked up from their back-breaking toil on the soil to see stately dignitaries setting up with practiced skill an imposing background of crimson robes, black-robed attendants, vellum-bound books—awe-inspiring ceremony and ritual. Against this they moved with the quiet dignity of men used to unquestioned authority. They represented the legal masters of the Basques, the Kingdom of France. Their very presence filled the thoughts and colored the imagination of the humble, poor, illiterate population made up just then of the most nervously impressionable part of any population, the women, the children, the old and the sick.

The courts, like our present-day courts, were well and efficiently organized, and moved forward into action with the disciplined certainty of seasoned troops advancing over familiar ground. They were experienced men who knew the resources of their profession, just as competent cross-examining lawyers do nowadays. They knew just what to do and how to do it, how to start with little and make it more, what forcing-bed to provide for hysteria, how to propagate insanity, grafting it from the weak upon the strong, as clever horticulturists propagate fruit-grafts—all this, you must not forget, just like any of our present law-courts, with the single-minded intention of causing truth to prevail and justice to be done.

Looking the ground over, they carefully picked their first case. In Bayonne for half the year and in the village of Ascain for the other half, lived an old ecclesiastic, a canon of the Cathedral, a doddering ancient, well known to every one in the region. He was nearer ninety than eighty, very infirm both in body and mind. He was a familiar figure as he tottered about on the arm of a silent, elderly serving-man, or sat wearily, sometimes weeping from senile fatigue, through the long services in the Cathedral. He was so forgetful and incapable that he had not for years dressed himself without help, and he had long ago ceased to distinguish the faces of people perfectly well known to him. As his bewilderment of mind increased he had begun an odd habit of accosting children who passed him on the street, calling them by names which were not theirs, and saying that they were his grandchildren. "That is Elias, my son Robert's boy," he would say; or, "Suzanne, you look just as your mother, my daughter, did at your age." The children used to receive these remarks sometimes with embarrassed giggles, sometimes with the indifference of long usage. Their mothers, who had seen many other feeble old people, thought nothing of it save that one or two of the more sensitive imaginative ones pitied the childless old man for these pathetic betrayals of the loneliness of his celibate life.

Now it seemed—rumors flared up from one remote hamlet to another, like signal lights—it seemed that the court of great and wise judges at St. Jean-de-Luz had brought before them the little scullery maid of the old canon's house, a white-faced adolescent orphan called familiarly "Jeanne Twitch-fast" because of a nervous spasmodic flicker of her left cheek and eyelid. Jeanne had testified, it was said, first nothing more than that the old housekeeper was very cross to her, that she had been forced to scrub floors, and was not given nice things to eat. But under expert cross-examination, she soon began to report other matters, strange sounds and sights in the old canon's house.

Had she, she was asked, ever noticed for instance that after the old housekeeper had gone to bed, the broom was missing from the kitchen hearth?

Jeanne turned her twitching yellow-white face up earnestly to the learned man interrogating her and after a long gaze into his expectant eyes, did remember. . . . "Why, yes, yes. The broom often *was* gone at night."

"And not returned till morning?"

"Yes, yes," Jeanne nodded a great many times, her eyes never leaving those of the examiner, "yes, just as the gentleman said, the broom was not there till morning."

The examiner dropped his voice four or five notes to a rich dark tone. "And . . . perhaps . . ." his keen masterful eyes drove deep into hers, "perhaps much worn then, as though it had been much used?"

238

"Yes, yes, yes, yes," said Jeanne, nodding. She caught her breath, she put her hand to her head and caught at the table as though she were dizzy. "Yes, so it was! Much worn, with . . . with strange marks on the handle." Here a movement in the court-room, a leaning towards her of learned men. ". . . strange marks . . . like . . . like . . . as though a great beast had been worrying it."

"A-a-ah!" There was a great noting down on tablets on the part of the red-robed judges. This was new, something fresh to vary the stale old routine, something different to report later to other judges from courts of other regions, in dinner-table reviews and comparisons of cases. "As though a great beast had been worrying it." They repeated the phrase, they noted it down, it passed from mouth to mouth till it reached the door-keeper who, translating it into Basque, reported it in a whisper, behind his hand, to the idlers loitering about the door. Jeanne in the meantime, her eyelid twitching fast, went on with her answers to those creative questions—"Yes, there *was* a goat-like smell about the house, sure enough."

"Yes, she had been wakened by strange noises often."

"Yes, she had looked through a crack in the door and had seen . . ."

"Yes, the silent old serving-man, too . . . and yes, now she thought of it, the old canon . . ." Her breath came fast, her knees shook so that she could scarcely stand, her face was whiter all the time . . . yes, she remembered . . . she had seen . . . she had heard . . . they had said . . . they had done . . .

Her answers, set down in writing by the learned judges, were passed from mouth to mouth till they reached the door-keeper and the group at the door.

By the next day not a remote farmstead in the region but had heard that the old canon and his serving-man and his housekeeper had been arrested on Jeanne's testimony and taken to St. Jean-de-Luz for examination. The discovery had been made, it seemed, that the whole household had been under the protection of Jaun Gorri, whose other name was Satan . . . who through them had been stealthily stretching out his talons over all the region. The tears of the old man when he sat through the long church services had not at all been tears of fatigue and old age, but of anger at the holy symbols around him. Every night he and the old housekeeper burst from the upper window of the house, bestriding the same broom, their skirts indecently tucked up, and flew off to orgies with other devotees of the Evil One . . . and *oh!* worst of all, that mania of his for calling little boys and girls his grandchildren and giving them strange names . . . that, it seemed, was a formula of black magic, a Satanic rechristening of harmless innocents, a dedication of helpless little ones to the service of wrong and wickedness. Those learned men had recognized it at once, from their deep study of the powers of evil, as a well-known device of Satan to get young souls into his clutches.

Whatever may have been thought of these first revelations by people in general, the ever-fearful hearts of the mothers of young children were pierced clear through by the danger to their little sons and daughters. It made, I gathered, the same sort of cyclone explosion which would be made nowadays by a rumor that a wicked old man had been handing out to children diphtheria germs hidden in candy. The Cathedral quarter of Bayonne and all the countryside near Ascain, seethed with hysteria. Nothing else was talked of, could be talked of. The Cathedral was stormed, even at the hours of the saying of Mass, by distracted women bringing in frightened screaming children to be exorcised by priestly prayers and freed by holy-water from the horrible danger which lay over them. One poor mother whose only child, a gentle little girl, had fallen ill and died shortly after an encounter with the old canon, lost her mind in agony about the dead child's soul, rushed screaming to the river and flung herself in. She was rescued, and told it was her duty to other mothers and other children to live and testify in court as to the details of her poor child's sickness and death. She did testify. . . .

One woman there was who kept her head, a mother, too, whose four sons had often been noticed by the canon. This was Dominiqua Hiriart, called Dominiqua Dargaineratz from the name of her husband's ancestral home where she lived, a sober, middle-aged respectable farm-woman, who had for years supplied the canon's household with butter and cheese. She had no more education or information than any other of the over-worked, unled, superstitious, impressionable, lonely Basque women of that region. But her heart was fed from some inner source of sanity, and through strange ways, as you will see, had strange and great effects as even one such heart always has. When her two younger sons, Andech and Manech, came bursting in, gray with

terror at the possibility that their souls had been de-
livered over to Jaun Gorri, or Satan, as the French
called Beelzebub, their mother turned from her churn
to laugh at them. Then, sobered by the sight of their
shaking knees and trembling white lips, she rose, and
putting a hand on a shoulder of each, told them quietly
that their souls were safe as long as they were good
boys. And because she was what she was, they believed
her.

Dominiqua was the only woman in a household of
seven men, four sons, her husband, her old father and
an unmarried uncle who lived with her. They were all
strapping brave men too, even the two boys, fourteen
and seventeen, left at home by the fishing-fleet because
of their youth. But Dominiqua was easily the strongest-
hearted of the family and they all knew this. Hers was
the voice of authority in that house. Her boys had but
to look into her steady eyes to forget their panic. The
color came back into their wild young faces, they drew
a long breath or two, and the horror was behind them,
locked out of the house so filled with their mother's
personality that there was no room left in it for hysteria. From that day on she kept them with her, forbidding their going near the court of St. Jean-de-Luz

or listening to the stories told about the doings there. Her old father and her uncle, a younger man, who had broken his leg just before the sailing of the fishing-fleet and so had been left at home, came and went on the necessary errands, and supplied the household with fish of their own daily catching in the Bay.

All this time the old canon was being examined, his dulled ears catching what blurred notion they could of the questions put to him, his maundering answers all noted down, his head held up by attendants so that his bleared eyes might face one witness after another; failing in strength from one day to the next till he could no longer walk but was carried into the court-room in a chair, his bald unreverend head wagging feebly from one shoulder to the other like a broken-necked old doll's.

Day by day all that he said, all that his serving-people said, was repeated far and wide with all the trimmings of verbal reports, with the many distortions that go with translations into another tongue, for almost none of the Basques of that period spoke French or understood it. Finally it was reported that the net had closed about him, that the serving-man and the house-keeper (promised immunity as mere accomplices if they would confess) had told the truth about their master's inner life, had told all . . . the Basque country turned cold to hear that all.

The execution of the old canon was another well-directed attack on the general mental equilibrium. Manifestly unaware of what was going on around him, he was half dragged, half carried into the open square at the side of the Cathedral, his canonical vestments stricken from him with impressive ceremonies of condemnation, and his withered body, nearly lifeless already with age and exhaustion, was tied to a stake and burned to death.

The savage sights and sounds of this spectacle had upon the nerves of the crowd of spectators somewhat the same maddening searing effect as . . . let us say . . . a lynching nowadays. They dispersed, some sobbing, some silent and rigid as stone, some faint and pale, others with swollen and congested faces, all half crazed with excitement.

All, that is, with the exception of the dignitaries of the Bordeaux Courts of Sorcery, for whom this was an expected incident in the well-known routine of their profession.

They expected, also, the flood of reports of other

cases of witchcraft which poured in on them immediately after the public execution. Just as they thought, those Basque women were in league with the devil. It had been going on for years, unsuspected, unrepressed, till their Gallic acumen had detected it and their professional diligence set itself the task of rooting it out. These wanton women had run wild as all women would, left without men to command them. For a time the court was a mere welter of investigation . . . every judge's hand ached with noting down testimony about suspected witches. Every neighborhood, it now seemed, had had some strange personality whose oddities or whose unaccountable undeserved success in life or whose original turn of mind had escaped comment until the learned French lawyers had come with their explanation, with this all-explaining key to mysteries.

The very night after the execution of the wicked old canon, the powers of Evil had multiplied themselves, had come out in the open as never before. Many of the people who had been present (you must remember here that Dominiqua had kept her household away from that sight), reported that Satan had taken advantage of their helplessness in sleep and had invaded their very bedrooms with his solicitations to vileness.

In many cases he had taken care to strengthen his appeal by bringing with him one of his devotees, some neighbor or acquaintance known to the sleeper. These allies of the goat-footed messenger from hell told in glowing words of the marvelous bodily joys and worldly advantages they had won by giving themselves up to all-powerful Evil. Sometimes these nocturnal friends of Satan were queer old women, living alone and already looked upon a little askance. Sometimes on the contrary they were beautiful women surrounded by their little children, with every appearance of virtue. In this manner one withered unmarried woman, lame and bent with spinal trouble, learned in a vision that a girlhood rival of hers, now a young matron, to all appearances devout and harmless, drew from nocturnal orgies with Beelzebub the unnatural strength which enabled her to work and prosper beyond others, and in her youth had sucked up from the same infamous source the hateful beauty which had dazzled young men, which had witched a sweetheart away from the lame girl with the crooked spine.

These stories, naming names, with circumstantial details, were told through an interpreter to the French lawyers at St. Jean-de-Luz. With no need of an interpreter, they flared redly up and down the rocky paths of all that region. Many people believed them at once. Why, yes, of course, it was the simple obvious explanation for many unaccountable things. This must be the reason why old Granny Elissamburu managed somehow to live, although everybody knew she had scarcely a penny. This must be why young Juanech Etchahoun had to the dismay of his family turned away from a prosperous sweetheart to the daughter of a poor and landless farm-hand. This explained why the hail storm which had beaten down all the crops of the farmers near Urrugne had left those of Maï Urabayen; why the Lhande flocks never had sickness even when the scab took toll of all other sheep; now it was plain why the third Iztueta child was so twisted and crippled—the devil was his father, not old Iztueta at all; now people knew what old Aunt Gachucha had been up to when she was seen hobbling back to her cabin at four in the morning.

There were, of course, a few stiff-necked, opinionated people, Dominiqua Dargaineratz among them, who professed some incredulity, tried to pooh-pooh the excitement. At once these became (if we will look back into the spy-mania period of our late war experience, this will seem quite natural) objects of suspicion them-selves, probably secret friends of the demon.

But more proof was soon forthcoming, proof enough to stagger any doubt. Satan grew bolder, cynically un-ashamed—showed himself leaping and dancing like a hairy goat to frighten little girls watching the sheep in lonely pastures. Stood like a horned shadow chuckling in corners of the cow-barns, scaring the boys away from their milking. Left behind him his strong musky odor . . . sweeter than roses to his followers, it was said . . . in dairies, so that no cleaning or airing freed the milk of it. Finally thrust his way, hideously in-visible, into lighted rooms, ruffling up the hair of a horrified shrieking girl, laying a burning finger on the cheek of a child clutched close in his mother's arms.

The lawyers at St. Jean-de-Luz were the only peo-ple in the region not at all surprised by these doings. Taught by long professional experience, they had or-ganized themselves in expectation of it, as a good doctor prepares for the next phase in the malady he is treating. Hardly a detail of it was unfamiliar to them. They worked long and hard in the next days, sparing no time and effort to protect these defenseless country people. Testimony was taken all day long. Even so there were always white-cheeked people waiting in the anteroom, rehearsing to each other in whispers the stories they had come to tell, or passing on to others what they had learned of the possibilities of witchcraft from the talk of learned lawyers overheard in the court-room on previous days.

The taking of testimony began to be alternated with long cross-examining séances with the accused persons themselves, who, having been brought in from their homes, were not allowed to return, were kept in solitary custody, seeing no one but their jailers and the judges before whom they passed for a rigorous daily interrogation.

The well-trained orderly minds of the lawyers soon began to arrange all this heaped-up incoherent material in a lucid chronological statement. With scholarly exactitude the precise date of Satan's arrival in person in the Basque country was discovered and set down. The statistics of growth of his dark dominion were accurately calculated. The exact spot (anybody in that region will point it out to you) became known to which night after night he summoned the members of his accursed confraternity. The summit of La Rhune, bald, wind-swept, overlooking both sea and mountains, was

where he stood, watching his acolytes streaming towards him through the darkened midnight skies. People
told of having seen these dreadful revels, of recognizing behind goat-skins and under horns the faces and
forms of their neighbors as they pranced about Jaun
Gorri, the Red Lord, who stood in their midst smoking
and flaring like a bonfire.

One little fifteen-year-old dairy maid told in detail
of her adventure. A neighbor (whom she named) had
urged that she go only once to see it and learn for herself of the new powers it would confer on her. Told
that she must not utter one word of any sort, no matter
what she saw, she went flying off on a broom with the
neighbor to the top of La Rhune. To the lawyers at
St. Jean-de-Luz she described what and whom she
saw there, down to the last detail of matted hair,
flushed maniac face, and exposure of goat-shaped
legs.

She had heard in these last weeks so many detailed
descriptions of these revels that it was about what she
expected; nothing surprised her; nothing drew from her
a murmur until she saw with her own eyes among the
dreadful creatures worshiping Evil, her own employer,
decent, middle-aged Dominiqua Dargaineratz. At this

she forgot herself, clasped her hands and cried out in stupefaction, "Oh, holy Jesu!" Whereat instantly everything had disappeared into blackness, she had been horribly tumbled about, bruised and beaten and finally flung with a malignant bone-breaking violence back into her own bed at home.

The next day Dominiqua Dargaineratz was taken down to the Court at St. Jean-de-Luz for examination.

III

When the grandfather and uncle returned from their day's fishing they found the boys half demented with sorrow and rage, stunned by their helplessness before the ten black-robed guards who had suddenly appeared with a cry of "Summons for Dominiqua Dargaineratz!" She had been allowed no time to collect her mind, usually so quiet and orderly, no time to advise her boys what to do, even if she had known what to tell them. The guards had closed in on her and moved away. Weeping aloud . . . their strong, self-possessed mother *crying* . . . she had disappeared.

The four Dargaineratz males held a horrified council of war in the cold deserted kitchen of the farmhouse, the grandfather sixty-seven years old but still

hale and sound, the uncle a vigorous man of forty-
eight with his broken leg still in splints, the two half-
grown boys. These last had but one thought, a senseless
childish idea born of their utter ignorance of the great
world . . . if only Father were here! And Gratien,
the broad-shouldered older brother, then in the magnificent vitality of his twenty-three years, and Pedro
the oldest brother, strongest of them all. Nobody
would *dare*, if the men were at home.

Standing by the fireless hearth, the grandfather and
uncle listened with grave pale faces to the story told
by the frantic boys. They had not been weakened and
crazed by the prevailing madness, you must remember,
because Dominiqua had stood between them and belief
in it. In their minds now there was nothing but a rage
of wrath at the danger to her, to all their countryside.
They looked at each other. Yes, the boys were right
they thought. The men ought to be told what was
happening. Those ignorant rustic simpletons, though
adult men, were not more learned in worldly wisdom
than the adolescents, shared their lack-witted delusion
that mere manhood could stand up against the might
and majesty of accepted law. They too knew less than
nothing of how things go in the great world. To

them as to the boys there came no vision of the pitiful helplessness of a handful of ignorant fishermen
against the crushing power of a great state enforcing
its authority.

Yes, if only the men were at home . . . !

But this was in late June. The earliest return from
the Banks ever known was in early October. There was
no faintest possibility of reaching them before that,
was there?

*Was there?*

Two of the four gathered together in that stricken
home were boys; of the two men one was an old man,
the other was on crutches. But they both knew how to
handle a boat as other men know how to walk and
breathe. Both for many years had made the cross-
Atlantic trips to the Banks, and the older man was
what the Basques of that period called a "navigator,"
that is, he had been one of the council of elder seamen
who year after year had steered the fishing fleet to its
destination with no other aid than a rough chart, a
compass, the stars and a homemade rule-of-thumb
method of dead reckoning.

The old man and the crippled man looked long into
each other's faces, while the two boys dashed angry

tears from their eyes to watch their elders, and held
their breath to catch the first word which would break
that silence.

IV

The long, hectic weeks after Dominiqua's arrest
went by like the timeless nightmare days and nights of
a delirious man sick with a fever. The lawyers, physi-
cians to this sickness trained in the tradition of the
malady, treated it with skill, applying to each stage
exactly the maneuvers best fitted to it. For a long time
there were no formal judicial trials, such as had re-
sulted in the execution of the old canon. There were
only investigations. The accused women were merely
kept in custody, cut off from their homes, their children, their old people, their sick, and from the daily
work on the soil, in the house, in the herds, which supplied the food for those dependents. Every day these
ignorant, simple, superstitious creatures were brought
before the disciplined minds of their judges and closely
questioned. That was all.

And that was enough. The judges knew very well
that these wild-eyed, ignorant, haggard country women
would not prove difficult cases. For most of them, the
mere deadly daily draught of homesickness would be

enough, all that was needed to bring them to a proper sense of their sins.

This was true even of those brought in early in the proceedings, in June, before the matter was really under way. Two months later, by the end of July, things had progressed so that such accused women were almost ripe for the last questionings, racked as they were, as every one was, by the horrors constantly revealed, shocked by the appalling details dragged by cross-examination from witnesses. Many of these details were of a gross violence unheard of by ignorant virtuous women who had passed from their parents' homes to those of their husbands, most of whose lives were absorbed in the harmless doings of little children. Only to hear such beastliness named aloud unhinged their minds. Morbidly fascinated by the abomination, they brooded over it, gazed into the darkling mirror of these new polluting conceptions. When suddenly from out that troubled glass their own distraught faces looked palely back at them, it was as though a strangling hand had closed about the neck of a dove. The mad flutter of wings could last but a moment. The result could be in no doubt to any experienced observer.

Not, of course, literally in every single case were

such women ripe for the last questionings. Two recal-
citrants were discovered very soon. Dominiqua Dargaineratz and Gratiane Larramendi, the beautiful
proud girl of Urrugne. The evidence against them piled
higher and higher. Dominiqua's enviable success in
cheese-making, calf-raising, and managing her sons,
was plainly shown to depend on an unnatural alliance
with the devil. As to Gratiane, it now appeared that it
had long been an open secret in Urrugne that she must
be an adept in the foulest black arts, or she could not
so continually charm other girls' sweethearts away
from old loyalties.

And yet neither woman would admit guilt, although
all the usual irresistible pressure from the court was
brought to bear on them. Dominiqua quietly and
soberly denied every charge made against her and in
the intervals of her examinations fingered her rosary
and murmured her prayers. Gratiane denied the accusa-
tions with a scornful laugh and a flash from her eyes
which startled the jury of middle-aged and aging men
and stirred their blood.

As the weeks went on, the tremors caused by the execution of the old canon were dying down. It was
deemed expedient to push Gratiane's case out of its

turn, from the stage of cross-examination into the solemn ordeal of trial. She still callously protested her innocence, sustained no doubt by secret visits of Satan to her cell. She was condemned to death and burned to death on the square of her own village . . . just under the sun dial on the church tower which to this day looks down gloomily proclaiming in carven letters as it did over Gratiane's funeral pyre,

"Vulnerant omnes: ultima necat."
(Every one wounds: the last one kills.)

Gratiane's last hour is not forgotten. She died as proudly as she had lived, meeting death with her head held high under its fatal crown of beauty. It is told of her that the executioner "seeing her so beautiful and fresh, asked, as she went to her death, for a kiss from the lips which had so many times kissed those of Satan." She said nothing but she turned on him so burning a look of contempt that the memory of its fearlessness still flames on in the old stony village square where she died, three hundred years ago.

Immediately after this event, viewed by a large crowd, while the echoes from it were still quivering, the judges at St. Jean-de-Luz began a new procedure, familiar to them, but new to this inexperienced region, a whip-sawing on alternate days between threats of bringing the accused definitely to trial, and tempting promises of pardon even for full-fledged witches, if full confession were made and penance done. It was not long before the first confession was made . . . a hair-raising one, every unclean detail of which was noted down by the judges and scattered broadcast like wind-blown seed. Other confessions followed. The women who made them were not released but kept in custody till the day of penance. Talk began to circulate of what that penance would be. Some had heard that the confessed wretches would be made to walk in a procession of disgrace, candle in hand, barefooted, hair unbound, naked save for a short chemise, all the fifteen stony miles from St. Jean-de-Luz to the Cathedral at Bayonne. Others added that once there they would be forced to make the tour of the Cathedral on their bare knees, and then, stretched on the ground, to allow the men and women whom they had bewitched to trample back and forth over their bare flesh.

The Court at St. Jean-de-Luz worked faster and faster now. The metal was heated, those expert smiths of the mind knew that the hour for ringing blows had come. All this wave of collective hysteria had been plotted by their seasoned experience to its last curve. They could have made out a chart foretelling almost every detail of what would now happen. Confessions, many confessions. They felt an agreeable stirring of the blood at the thought of them. And after the confessions —rather quickly after, for the reaction from the fever sometimes set in rapidly—executions of the worst offenders. And after the executions, the long ceremony of penance full of savory details of personal degradation. Then a comfortable return to Bordeaux and a period of well-earned repose after work soundly and thoroughly carried through. It would be long, they felt, before witchcraft would raise its head in the Basque country again. At least it would be quite a while before another trial would be advisable.

Everything moved forward according to their schedule. Dominiqua Dargaineratz still stood stubborn. But other women confessed. Day after day the red-clad judges sat, their half-circle of scarlet flaring around some shrieking woman whose cries could be heard even out on the street where sickened listeners leaned faintly against the walls to hear. "That is Yoanna Yturbe's voice! She is confessing. Whom will she name as complice?" No need now for black-robed attendants to pass on the news to the door-keeper.

Day after day? No. For only three days did this phase last. On the fourth an old seaman, half blind and half deaf, looked up from where he was sadly mending a net on the beach of the port, looked up and dropped his nets in terror. He, the poorest, the wretchedest of the poor, was still not so negligible as to escape the roaming malignancy of Satan. He too was bewitched out of his true senses. For he seemed to see out at sea, their sails full set, driving straight towards the harbor—he saw—and yet this was not October, was not even September, was only the end of August, when the men of the fleet were half around the world—no, he had not seen them—no, he was bewitched—or he had so longed to see the men that he dreamed them.

But he could not take his eyes from those driving sails . . . well he knew every hull there . . . in many of them he had sailed. They were nearer now. They were at the entrance of the little port. He could see the black dots of the men on the decks, as they stood to the ropes. They were nearer. Or was it that he had run madly out into the water towards them? Shoulder deep he stood . . . straining his eyes, thinking he had died, or had become some one else . . . they were near now . . . he *could* see them.

The sails went rattling down to the decks . . . the swift small ships were sweeping on their impetus past him towards the inlet, towards the landing-place, they were real . . . he was alive . . . he was not crazy . . . *the men* . . . *the men were back!*

He shouted and screamed and waved his arms like a maniac. But not a man on any ship turned a head towards him. Their eyes were fixed on their goal, the Court House of the city.

By the time he had stumbled crazily out of the water and had run shrieking to the landing-place the ships were there, clustered thickly at haphazard on the water; the streets leading to the inlet were filled with hurrying people shouting to each other and waving their arms to the sailors. They, boat-hooks in hand, were swarming from one ship to another and so out on the land, those brawny, hard, deep-chested seamen, mighty as an incoming tide, their bold weather-beaten faces darkened by sun and wind, darkened still more by fury, fierce faces filled with the vitality of anger.

They swept up the street, and it was as though a sea-wind had burst upon the town and was racing before them, scouring out the stagnant air. The people who fell in behind that forward charge, swelling it to hundreds, the old men, the boys, the children, sobbed loudly and cried out greetings each to his own. But that swift phalanx of outraged manhood was silent.

The streets of the compact little town are not long, and the public square where the Court House stands is not far from the wharf. Never far, and that day so close at hand that by the time the black-cloaked French attendants had come to the doors, curious in their dignified official way as to the meaning of that sudden swift thunder of trampling feet, the whirlwind was upon them. It swept across the square, swept them off their feet and burst with a roar into the courtroom.

These twenty-four learned and subtle-minded judges, they whose very names had turned cheeks pale with terror, wrapped in fine scarlet and rich ermine, symbols of their high station, their impregnable power . . . what were they now but twenty-four flabby paunchy men, feeble and horribly frightened. They knew no Basque, but there was no need of the court interpreter to make clear the meaning of those infuriated men who plucked them bodily from their chairs and flung them from calloused tarry hand to hand towards the door.

One of the dignitaries, one of the oldest and feeblest, too, kept his head a little, resisted, struggled, called out for the interpreter, tried with all the righteousness of his clear legal conscience to justify himself and all he stood for. "Tell them!" he shouted to the interpreter. "Tell them that their women have *confessed*. We are not responsible. They themselves have confessed to having commerce with the devil. It is nothing we have done. Tell them that Yoanna Elissamburu, that Maï Urabayen, that Madeleine Iztueta have freely confessed . . . tell their husbands that. That dozens of women have freely borne witness. . . ." Somehow, through the struggle and uproar of angry voices, the terrified interpreter, half-mechanically obedient to the old authority, shrieked this out till it came to the ears of the husbands of the women named. For the space of a breath they stopped stock-still, petrified with astonishment. But what in an instant succeeded astonishment on their faces was not the expression of loathly, creeping panic-struck horror which the judges confidently expected on human faces as the reflection of their words. No, it was rough, hot-tempered masculine

264

impatience with female foolishness which burst out in their ejaculations: "My wife said she was a witch? The *idiot!* I'll take care of her!"

"Yoanna pretending to be in league with Satan? I'll beat her till she can't stand."

"Wait till I get my hands on Maï. I'll teach her to know what's what! I know what my own wife is, I should hope."

"If there's anything the matter with my Madeleine, I don't need any old man in a black gown to tell me what to do."

All this a momentary eddy in the tidal wave of passion which swept those black and red-and-ermine chips helplessly out of the Court House, along the street and out of the city. What were they after all, what had they ever been, but four and twenty men, like any men, but less vigorous? Even the weedy half-grown boys in the streets perceived this now and laughed to see the terror on those greenish indoor faces.

For the judges were certain that their last hour had come, that the mob, the low ignorant many-headed which always hates superior knowledge and learning, would actually do them to death. But the Basques had but one demand to make of them—to get out, go where they belonged and never come back. Just that natural reasonable demand. Some jowls may have received resounding slaps, some reverend ears may have been emphatically boxed, some obese bodies jostled and shaken and bruised, but when the huddled group of red and black cloaks found themselves on the road outside the city, there was not a broken bone among them.

Behind them in the street stood a crowd of brawny Basques, laughing in spite of their anger at the discomfited woman-frighteners. "They look like draggle-tailed old roosters!" cried a little boy's high voice.

This was what was behind them. Before them stretched the long stony fifteen miles to Bayonne, over which they had purposed to send those naked helpless disgraced women.

You know which way they went.

v

Behind them, so the old phrase has come down, "the whole town rang to the sound of exasperated men beating their wives," and to the long bursts of wild healing tears with which those hysteric women, thus roughly treated to what is still a sovereign cure for hysteria, awoke from their nightmare. They came to themselves

266

as people emerging from a delirium, and each found herself blessedly just what she had always been, the wife of Gratien or Manech or Manuel, the mother of little Gachucha—"Hasn't *any*body remembered to comb her hair since I was home!"—or the twins— "How *long*, I should like to know, since those children have had their feet washed!"—the owner and care-taker of peaceable dependent cattle and sheep— "Oh, old Lalli has calved and nobody at home to look out for the calf . . . *and a heifer*, too!" and "St. Michael defend us, look at the dirt on the dairy floor!"

The old sweet, heavy, steadying responsibilities, affections, burdens, cares, anxieties, satisfactions, took up their old homes in the new-garnished chambers of those minds swept clean of mania by the ungentle good sense of their husbands.

In short, there was, just as the learned judges had predicted, not a witch left in the Basque country.

And that's really all there is to the story. Except the part which boys like best to hear about, the adventuring of the little half-provisioned, quarter-manned ship with the two half-men and the two boys, which went all across the summer Atlantic to take the news to the men. With what gusto those scenes are retold! The battering gale they weathered in the midst of the voyage, their dogged hanging to the wheel though dead for sleep, the incredible morning when they saw land and knew they had won through. The arrival of the weary little ship on the Newfoundland coast, finding the fishermen of the fleet half on and half off the land, curing codfish in the sun. Their astonishment, alarm, and at once, like the bursting out of flame, their fury! Their starting up as though they had trodden on a serpent, and taking to their own ships in such haste that they stopped not to gather together the odds and ends of tools and clothing left on shore. And the exciting days and nights of the race back across the sea, every sail set, every eye strained ahead till the well-known coast was in view, and then the maneuvering to gather all the ships together for that rushing entrance into the old harbor. To this day, Basque boys look wistful as they think of the good fortune of Andrech and Manech Dargaineratz in the midst of all that. It is their opinion that boys nowadays don't have any luck!

There is another part of the story which would perhaps not interest a boy, about which in fact nobody ever told me a word, but which is my favorite scene. This is the reunion of Dominiqua Dargaineratz and her menfolks. I won't try to describe to you as I see it the meeting of those strong men with the maker of the home which had given them their strength, because I always get very excited when I think about it and can't find any words but exclamations. I leave you to imagine it for yourself.

Are you interested in hearing what became of the judges? I can tell you. That is part of what has come down by oral tradition quite differently from what was written by the counselor. When they reached Bayonne, their jelly-like muscles aching under the weight of their overfed, underworked bodies, they were forcibly reminded not only that Bayonne is a walled and fortified town but that it is a Basque town. The city gates were closed. No one came to open to their knocking. Among the tired drooping group of notable lawyers, some one put falteringly the question, "How far is it to Bordeaux?"

Well, helped by casual shepherds on the Landes, and by occasional travelers, ultimately they straggled back on foot into their own world. And then what? How about the might, majesty and dignity of constituted legal authority? How about the pitiful helplessness of a handful of ignorant fishermen against the power of a great nation? That was what those judges wanted to know. It was also what I wanted to find out, three centuries later. Why hadn't it worked out according to formula?

I made little progress for some time. My Basque narrators had a true whole-hearted Basque indifference to what happens outside their world. All that I could get from them was the vague outline of a story of not unfamiliar red-tape official lethargy. The judges put in report after report, but nobody at headquarters did anything. They were not as a matter of fact very much beloved in their own city. Why would they be? The news of their treatment at the hands of the Basque fishermen got around to the tune of delighted laughter from men who would not have dared to look a sorcery expert in the face. The reports of the outrage were then filed in Paris, where the judges' story was listened to, although without any warm outpourings of sympathy, for it seems that although they were very powerful, the members of the Courts of Sorcery were naturally not very popular with other learned professions, any more than spies, detectives and police captains are social favorites in our own day. Time went on. Other things happened.

Little by little dust gathered on the reports. Other far more important and exciting matters occupied French officialdom. There seemed to be nothing else for me to discover. And yet I could not but feel that there must have been some hidden spring which I had missed.

My questionings went for naught till the day when somebody's very old great-aunt said that, now I mentioned it, it seemed as though she had heard in her youth a report of something that somebody, very old then, had said about something or other said by Henry Fourth (yes, he of the white plume and of Navarre), then King of France.

And what had this been? A long stirring in dusty memories brought out little by little the tradition that Henry had been enchanted with the story of the impious disbelief in sorcery of those ignorant codfishers, and fell into fits of laughter when the indignant report of the outrage came to his attention.

"*Ventre St. Gris!* Fishermen! And armed with nothing but boathooks!" he was wont to cry delightedly, when reminded of the insult to one of his most feared law-courts.

Finally he had ended the appeals to him by saying decisively one day, "I am a Béarnais boy, born and brought up in the Pyrenees alongside those Basques. I know them. There's no use trying to do anything with a Basque. Once they have settled that something ought to be done, they go ahead and do it. What keeps the rest of us from going ahead and doing what we know ought to be done? A thousand barriers we call law and public opinion and convention. Basques treat such barriers as if they were cobwebs."

He paused and fingered his graying beard. "Cobwebs. Just cobwebs," he murmured to himself.